She sensed that he stood behind her

His hands curved over her shoulders; his voice was whimsical and soft. "That must be an emotional sort of hospital you work for, Sister Maddern, if they encourage you to burst into tears when the going gets rough."

She protested fiercely, "I do not burst into tears," but she was careful to keep her head averted.

It was several seconds before she discovered she was holding her breath. And then she let it out, very slowly, very carefully, so that he would not guess the effect he was having on her.

He took his left hand from her shoulder and slid his arm over her breast and down until it encircled her waist. Then he pressed her slim body backward until it leaned against him. Her skin tingled at his touch. Was it her body that trembled, or was it his?

SAMANTHA HARVEY
is also the author of this
Harlequin Romance

2481—THE DRIFTWOOD BEACH

Many of these books are available at your local bookseller.

For a free catalog listing all titles currently available,
send your name and address to:

HARLEQUIN READER SERVICE
1440 South Priest Drive, Tempe, AZ 85281
Canadian address: Stratford, Ontario N5A 6W2

The Distance Man

by

SAMANTHA HARVEY

Harlequin Books

TORONTO • NEW YORK • LOS ANGELES • LONDON
AMSTERDAM • PARIS • SYDNEY • HAMBURG
STOCKHOLM • ATHENS • TOKYO • MILAN

Original hardcover edition published in 1982
by Mills & Boon Limited

ISBN 0-373-02522-X

Harlequin Romance first edition January 1983

CHAPTER ONE

Vienna Maddern drove her neat yellow sports car into the courtyard of the Adelaide suburban flats where she lived.

She glanced overhead at the red brick walls with their potted flowers waving bravely outside each window. Petunias and pansies, vibrant in the South Australian sunshine. Vienna looked at them gratefully.

It was good to be home. She had really dreaded this afternoon's visit to the small private hospital and nursing home where Evelyn Harryn had spent the last years of her life.

She shouldn't have felt so badly about it. Until six months ago, Vienna had been a member of the nursing staff; the hospital corridors were as familiar to her as the rooms she lived in.

Yet ever since Matron had telephoned to say that Evelyn had died quietly in her sleep, and would Vienna please call as soon as she could, Vienna found herself putting off the visit, knowing she needed time to get used to the idea of seeing another patient in the bed that had been Evelyn's.

Now it was over; and all Vienna had to remind her of Evelyn was the flat, brown-paper-wrapped parcel on the car seat beside her—the painting that had been Evelyn's only treasured possession.

Vienna picked up the package and stepped out of her car, and it was then she saw the other vehicle parked across the courtyard, black and sleek and gleaming in the pleasant afternoon sunshine. Neil Rensome's car!

She paused and studied it thoughtfully, a slight

frown between her wide, winged brows. Neil should
have been sitting in his office at the hospital,
behind the door marked Administrator. She had
looked for him there, wondering at his absence.

Matron had made quite a fuss about handing
over the picture, making a little speech about how
Vienna had made the old lady's failing life happy,
and Vienna found herself blinking back tears. She
had looked for a shoulder to cry on—Neil's shoulder—and when she opened his door and found him
missing, Vienna had controlled her tears and
walked dry-eyed out of the hospital. Whatever
could have brought him visiting at this time of the
day? He would be waiting inside her flat, of course.
He knew where she kept her spare key, and he
would let himself in.

Vienna tucked the parcel under her arm and
went slowly upstairs to the first floor landing. As
she expected, the door of her flat opened easily
when she pushed it. Neil lounged on the divan in
front of her television set. He had helped himself
to a cool drink from her refrigerator, and when
she glanced at the small table beside him she saw
that it held two empty glasses.

She looked around her curiously, but Neil
jumped to his feet and almost as if he followed her
glance at the second glass he announced quickly,
'You've had a visitor.'

Vienna looked at Neil with pleasure. She always
had, ever since that first day when she joined the
hospital staff and knocked, not without trepida-
tion, on the Administrator's door.

A secretary had admitted her, and Vienna walked
across the soft carpet to the enormous polished
desk and found herself looking incredulously at
one of the most attractive men she had ever seen.

She remembered wondering if everyone else responded as she had done; he was so incredibly good-looking that she always found herself taking that second, extra look.

Regular features, beguiling brown eyes, soft sweet mouth—surely there had to be a flaw somewhere. Nobody could look that perfect. But the flaw had never revealed itself.

Not yet, Vienna warned herself cautiously, and sighed. Because she could have done without the quiet, nagging doubt that refused to be silenced ever since the day Neil had allowed her to leave the hospital without quite managing to cover his relief.

Six months ago Dr Jason, one of the hospital doctors, had offered Vienna the job of caring for some of his private patients away from the hospital. When she mentioned it tentatively to Neil, he made no attempt to dissuade her. He had even seemed in some odd and disquietening way slightly pleased, as though their relationship might have been developing too fast for him, as if he might have been relieved to find a little distance between them.

Vienna had tried to push the hurtful thought away from her, but it lingered. Even now, it could hurt, but only when Neil was not close enough to reassure her.

He walked towards her now and kissed her, and it seemed to her that his greeting was unusually warm.

'Collected your picture, I see,' he commented affably.

'Yes. The poor old lady, I wish she hadn't worried——'

'Don't be silly. She always said you were to have

her precious picture, didn't she?'

Neil watched while Vienna unwrapped the painting, and when she stood it on top of a low cabinet, leaning it against the wall, he walked over and studied it intently.

'Old family home, wasn't it? No great shakes as a work of art. Sentimental value, I suppose.'

He'd seen it before, of course. Evelyn kept it always beside her bed: the simple painting of a long ranch-type homestead in an outback setting of red earth and scattered saltbush, its roof painted green to blend with the eucalyptus and other trees around it.

Vienna remembered Evelyn pointing to the title *Red Vistas* and the signature, Ralph Darcour, beneath it.

'My grandfather,' she had confided, with pride and wistfulness.

Surprised by Neil's interest in the picture, Vienna watched him a moment before she walked into the kitchen and plugged in the electric jug to make a cup of tea. When she came back into the room Neil stood in front of the painting as though it fascinated him.

Vienna wished she didn't feel so disquieted. She asked softly, 'Neil, what are you doing here in the middle of the afternoon? And who was my visitor?'

'Oh!' He flushed and looked at her quickly, then away again. 'Didn't Matron—oh no, of course she didn't—Well, it's like this, my pet. We had a solicitor chap at the hospital this morning, asking for you. Seems your favourite patient, Evelyn Harryn, had been the subject of a long, long search. She inherited a share in some property, a cattle station in the back of beyond somewhere. Half-share, actually.' He moved to the divan and twisted his empty glass a little selfconsciously on the table, without looking directly at Vienna. 'And as you happen to be her legal heir—heiress, I suppose—well, it comes to you.'

The handsome face was slightly flushed. He wasn't really confused, just a little bit selfconscious, trying hard to sound half amused and not terribly interested in what he was telling her. But a curious intentness flickered in his eyes, a kind of tension in the way he looked at her, as if he might have been nervous about her reaction.

Vienna said tersely, 'Oh, what nonsense! Evelyn wanted me to have the picture, that's all. I suppose she felt—well, at least it would be looked at sometimes instead of being packed away into a cupboard somewhere.'

'She left you everything, Vee. She got hold of one of those legal forms where you fill in names and other relevant information and get two people to witness it, and she left you everything she had.'

'Because that was all she owned—the painting.'

Neil's glance at Vienna was wary. Off duty today, instead of uniform she wore a cream suit with a gold and white patterned blouse, and small gold earrings. Her hair was deep night-black, lustrous and heavy, brushed back from her forehead in two dark wings, held in place by gold clips in a style that would have been severe except for the bouncy roll of curls on her shoulders.

She looked tiny and delicate and vulnerable, but Neil knew from past experience that the fragility was an illusion. When strength was needed, Vienna could produce it.

Today, there was an unusual shining in her eyes, as though tears might not have been far away. He watched her uneasily. He wasn't sure about the tears, whether they were really there. It wasn't like Vee to be emotional, and her large emerald-green eyes always held a luminous quality—a kind of inner shining that gave her heart-shaped face a look of dreaminess that belied her strength and efficiency.

Neil stirred restively. His expression had become oddly stubborn.

'So it turns out the picture wasn't all Evelyn owned, after all. Unknown to her there's been a massive search going on for months. Some old fellow, an elderly relative, I think, left his share in this property to Evelyn's mother, if she still lived, or to her children, of which there was only your Evelyn. It's complicated, but that's how it works out. Thanks to the way Evelyn filled in that will form, you've inherited half a cattle station.'

Vienna asked levelly, 'And who was my visitor? A solicitor?'

'Nope.' He watched her carefully. 'He's a distant relative of the old girl's, some fellow from outback—came to make an offer for your share in the property when everything is finalised. Reasonable offer, he called it, but I soon set him right about that.'

'You did?'

The jug made boiling noises and Vienna hurried into her kitchen to make tea and biscuits, and all the time her head was whirling.

She carried the tray with teacups and biscuits into the other room and put it down; then she drew a deep breath and said carefully,

'Look, Neil, I know you're considering my interests, and I appreciate your concern. But Evelyn made her will so she could leave me the picture.

Only the picture—you must realise that.'

She poured tea, and found to her horror that
her hand was shaking. Her voice had sounded
shrill. Surely she wasn't going to let this small confusion throw her off balance?

She set down the teapot, disciplined her voice,
and added firmly, 'I couldn't accept anything else.
It wouldn't be right. It wasn't what she intended at
all.'

'Oh, for heaven's sake——' Neil began testily,
then it seemed to Vienna he made a special effort
to hide his annoyance, and patted her shoulder
affectionately before accepting his cup of tea.

'You're impractical, Vee darling. You need
somebody to look after you—I always thought so.
Evelyn Harryn might have been bodyworn, but her
mind was sound as a bell. She knew what she was
doing.'

Neil's attractive lips curled into a resentful pout.

I'm going to offend him, Vienna told herself
numbly, and he'll go away and leave me for ever.
All because of that silly will——

Neil sugared his tea, not looking directly at her.

'Anyway, this bloke Darcour—the solicitor told
me at the hospital he was going to call at your flat,
so that's why I came around here as soon as I could
get away. I told him he'd have to make a better
offer than the one he made this afternoon, so he's
coming back to discuss it with us tonight.'

With *us*, Neil said. As though their relationship
were firmly cemented, and not the fragile affair she
had imagined it to be. She ought to have been
pleased, delighted, but all she knew was that a terrible feeling of misgiving had begun to push somewhere in the back of her mind, and that it grew
stronger with every word Neil said.

She went into the kitchen while Neil telephoned his mother to let her know he would be staying at the flat for dinner. Vienna tried hard not to listen, because Neil had always been so careful to keep them apart, her and his mother.

At the hospital, some of the nurses had laughed about it. Openly, at first.

'Aha! Just wait until he takes you home to meet his mother!'

Then secretly, their eyes expectant, waiting, sympathetic . . .

So Vienna busied herself while Neil talked. She heard him saying, 'Yes, Mother,' and, 'Of course, Mother,' as if he were not the brisk and capable administrator of a private hospital at all but merely a dutiful son placating an over-protective guardian; and her eyes widened in surprise.

Yet when he settled himself on the divan again, the whole idea seemed ridiculous, because he was a distinguished-looking and confident man and Vienna, along with most of the nursing staff, admired him tremendously.

She wondered whether she should try explaining to him again why she couldn't and wouldn't take advantage of Evelyn's well-meaning mistake and accept money from the country man for a share in some property she wasn't meant to have. The painting, yes. But half a cattle station—that was ridiculous.

She was appalled to find herself wishing Neil would go away and leave her to explain the situation to the man when he arrived. And, even more disturbing, she realised Neil was grimly determined to stay.

After dinner Vienna washed the dishes unhappily, and when everything was cleared away she went into her bedroom and freshened her face and brushed her hair. The eyes that looked back at her from the mirror were troubled.

Neil was an astute businessman, as well as an attractive companion, and he had made it plain that he wasn't going to see her fritter away a chance to make more money than had been offered. What he would say when he realised she had no intention of accepting a cent from the outback man who was coming to 'buy her out', Vienna shivered to think. But she wouldn't take advantage of the man, she told herself. She couldn't.

Replenishing her lipstick, she sighed miserably. This could very well be the end of her relationship with Neil. A man like Neil wasn't going to waste his time on a girl he considered stupid, un-businesslike and overly sentimental.

Vienna took off her cream jacket. The gold-patterned blouse with its long full sleeves and tight cuffs, the softly-tied neckline, looked fresh and smart; but for all that, she pulled a wry face at her reflection. This was going to be a difficult evening ... She wished she were better prepared.

When the chimes from her doorbell sounded, she moved to answer, but Neil was already there. Over-eager, suggested a small voice at the back of Vienna's mind, but she smothered it fiercely. She wasn't going to take advantage of a poor well-meaning cattleman, but neither was she going to criticise Neil unfairly. She stood beside the cabinet, watching Neil usher in her visitor.

She didn't know what she had expected. Slim-legged working jeans and spurred boots and open-necked checked shirt, perhaps. Maybe even a wide-brimmed hat ... Certainly nothing like the man who stalked coolly ahead of Neil into her lounge room and stared about him critically. At her cabinet with the painting on top of it, at her blue divan with its harlequin-coloured cushions and the rose-coloured curtains to match the floor rugs.

A little frivolous perhaps, a little like a teenager's room, if you wanted to be critical. But it was the ideal change of scene after the muted comfort, the sterile polish, of hospital wards.

Immaculately dressed in pearl-grey suit and lavender shirt, with soft rose and grey tie, the visitor surveyed her icily out of eyes only slightly greyer than his suit; distant eyes that probed, summing her up, missing nothing, and by the twist of his thin sardonic lips he wasn't exactly impressed by what he saw.

Only his face and hands suggested the country man. Face tanned Indian red-brown, with two hard lines from nose to mouth-corners, as though that craggy jaw had been hard-set so many times the imprint of strong will remained permanently etched there. Straight yellow hair, sunbleached in white and silver streaks; and a way of standing that spoke of power and authority.

Neil was no weakling, but beside him the grey-suited man towered broad-shouldered and unapproachable.

He said, 'Miss Maddern—Sister Maddern, I believe?' because Neil was a little slow about introductions. He spoke in a well-modulated voice that surprised Vienna. She knew it shouldn't have. The days of country bumpkins were long gone.

Neil interjected hastily, 'Vienna, this is Mr Darcour—Mr Brenden Darcour,' and Vienna said 'Hello', across a wall of hostility. He summed her up. Neatly and swiftly he put together the slight graceful figure, the heart-shaped face with its eyes of glowing green and the suggestion of vulnerability . . . he added them all up, and formed his own conclusions.

After Neil's hasty introduction the stranger did not hold out his hand. Even when he sat down on her most comfortable chair, leaving her and Neil to share the divan, he managed to remain aloof.

Neil offered drinks, but this time they were refused. He ostentatiously manoeuvred the small table, complete with ashtray, close to the man's right hand, but he did not use it.

Vienna thought, startled, 'He thinks Neil lives here. He thinks we're—what's the word—co-habiting . . .'

A nervous giggle died in her throat. Neil was letting him think so. Deliberately, he was taking over. It seemed so obvious the man from outback should have seen through it, but he didn't. Those impervious eyes flicked her, discarded her.

'Let's get down to business, shall we?'

His terseness shocked her—the hostility whip-lashing his voice. This man was rude; unbelievable, unreasonably rude!

Vienna said swiftly, coolly, 'We have no business to discuss, Mr Darcour. You didn't need to come here. You could have saved your time. Evelyn— Mrs Harryn—left me a painting——'

The keen grey eyes inspected her, this time with a faint gleam of what might have been interest. It soon disappeared.

He said curtly, 'This afternoon I made an offer for what will become your share of the Red Vistas property. Your—er—friend tells me you don't find it acceptable.'

Vienna broke in, daring him to continue, 'Evelyn left me her *painting*. I can't see what all the fuss is about.'

'She may have thought she was bequeathing you a painting,' Neil interrupted. 'Vienna, the legal position is——'

'Ah, yes!' The stranger could interrupt too. Mouth still curling in that hateful, arrogant message of disapproval, he interjected softly, 'The legal position, Miss Maddern, is that you will eventually inherit a half-share in Red Vistas. I am here to tender my offer for that share when the legal processes are concluded.'

'I don't want——'

'Oh, for heaven's sake, Vienna,' Neil turned on her impatiently, 'it's complicated enough already without you tossing spanners into the works!'

Brenden Darcour watched them with those penetrating eyes, not bothering to voice his frosty disapproval. If anything, Vienna thought, his reactions had become colder, even supercilious.

He repeated the offer he had made to Neil that afternoon and Vienna gasped at the amount, but Neil brushed it aside without even consulting her.

'You must realise,' he was informing the other man, 'there was a very special relationship between Vienna and your relative, Evelyn Harryn. Vienna is a particularly dedicated nurse.'

He made it sound nauseating, Vienna decided angrily—smug, and somehow insincere, like a sales pitch.

The man from outback must have thought so too, for he inclined his head coldly towards Vienna.

'A very rewarding occupation.' His voice was cynical. 'I trust you have your share of grateful patients.'

Vienna stared at him incredulously. So that was

what he was suggesting, that she'd wheedled her way into a patient's affection for what she could get! Her embarrassment was swept away in an uprush of anger.

'You didn't call to see her,' she flared at him. 'You didn't spare her a minute, did you? All those months, and not one visitor, not even a letter— nothing! How do you think she felt?'

Her face burned with anger. His, on the other hand, remained bland. His lips curled.

'How could I visit her? I belong to a very distant branch of the family. I didn't even know the woman existed.'

Instantly Vienna felt the heat of her anger turn to ice-coldness.

'Her name was Evelyn,' she rebuked him freezingly. 'Not—not—"the woman".'

He looked at her closely then. His expression remained totally remote, but when he spoke his voice was milder.

'Evelyn,' he amended.

'And you can keep——'

Neil broke in quickly. 'Vienna, Mr Darcour doesn't need you shouting at him.' He turned to Brenden Darcour with his hands spread palm-upwards in exaggerated apology. 'As you can see, Vienna is extremely upset—naturally. She was very, very fond of the old lady.'

If the other man waited for her to correct Neil, to snap at him that her name had been Evelyn, he waited in vain. A tide of feeling welled up in Vienna, a surge of grief and regret, and a sensation of bewilderment and outrage that the three of them should be here arguing about Evelyn's intentions, as though it had taken death to make anyone work up any sort of interest in her at all.

Neil had become persuasive. He was very good at it, Vienna was astonished to find herself deciding. He was experienced at handling people, and so he should be. Didn't he spend a part of every day soothing difficult patients and their sometimes equally difficult relatives, ironing out the small hostilities that occurred among staff, and generally making himself agreeable.

Now he turned his blandishments on to Brenden Darcour, and Vienna saw crossly that those cool inquisitorial grey eyes measured and discarded his peace efforts with a detachment that was almost totally rude.

'I'll tell you what I think, Mr Darcour. You're a reasonable man, I'm sure you'll understand. Before Vienna accepts this offer of yours, I believe she ought to have a look at the place. I mean, you can see we have no idea of its value.'

We, he was saying. The other man interrupted coldly.

'And just how do you propose to do that, Mr Rensome?'

'Quite simply. We'll drive up there and take a look around. I presume the place is accessible?'

'Just.'

'Then we'll go, as soon as possible. In fact——' Neil turned to Vienna smoothly, 'you're between cases now, aren't you? A break is just what you need. I can take a couple of weeks off. Matron and Katie, my secretary, can cover for me during that short time.'

He managed to make it sound as if any longer and the hospital would fall to pieces. He was being very pushy, Vienna thought disloyally. They were a great pair, the two of them, he and the man with the icy eyes.

She smoothed her hair back from her forehead in a graceful, nervous gesture, and glowered at them both, Neil with his smooth talk, the stranger with his watchful eyes, his distant manner.

The man in the grey suit stood up abruptly. 'I wouldn't recommend the trip,' he said. 'It's a rough road, the highway north.'

'It's sealed,' Neil argued swiftly. 'I've seen it——'

Brenden Darcour's voice was a biting drawl. 'Then you've seen the good part. The rest, as far as the turn-off to Red Vistas, is pretty rugged at present, I warn you.'

'But people do drive on it?'

He ignored that bit. He said, 'And you'd need to load up with provisions. The homestead hasn't been occupied for a while. There's not much in the way of facilities. I wouldn't attempt it, if I were you.'

Neil stood up, and Vienna wondered whether it was making him feel disadvantaged, to be seated with the other man towering over him. He said with determined brightness, 'We're not children, Mr Darcour, to be put off by a little inconvenience. I flatter myself I'm a competent driver.'

For the first time Brenden Darcour transferred his attention completely to Vienna, and the watchful eyes softened a little as if he might have been slightly amused. The eyebrows lifted, and Vienna wasn't sure whether his expression was derisive, or whether he asked a question. She forced herself not to look away, not to withdraw from that powerful, penetrating inspection.

Without any effort at all he was making her feel very uncomfortable. Then, with remarkable suddenness, the man in grey capitulated.

'There's nothing more to be said, then. I'm travelling north to my property in a couple of days' time. I'll pass the turn-off to Red Vistas. If you wish, you can follow me along the highway. You understand you must go well equipped? This is not a holiday resort you're visiting.'

Vienna stared at him in amazement. Had the man taken leave of his senses? She had no intention of accepting a share in Red Vistas, his 'reasonable offer' had been refused, and instead of arguing he was encouraging Neil in his wild scheme to travel outback.

Here she was, being manipulated by two men, neither of whom she liked very much at this moment, into taking a journey she'd no intention of taking. In fact, she hated the whole idea.

She opened her mouth to say so, and across the small room her visitor looked at her. It was a powerful look. Out of her anger, she tried to deflect his power; but he was, for some purpose of his own, ordering her to remain quiet.

Grey eyes narrowed, he stayed perfectly still, but being the man he was he made his message loud and plain. Perhaps he planned to trap them both in the coils of Neil's conniving. He looked capable of it. Whatever he had in mind, he said nothing, but the protests died on Vienna's lips, and she hated herself for her compliance.

Then Brenden Darcour turned away and spoke briefly to Neil. They were making arrangements over her head and around her, as if she were a child, not important enough to be consulted.

Neil said officiously, 'I think Mother should come with us. Naturally Vienna would prefer feminine company, and it's a long time since Mother had a holiday away from the city. I'm sure she

would enjoy it.' Vienna started to say no, but he
bustled on. 'My mother has relatives on the land
in West Australia—the Visetons. You may know
them.'

And once again Brenden Darcour looked at her
across the room, his sensuous mouth half twisted
with malice and amusement. He had grasped her
surprise and resentment. Deliberately, he looked
around the small flat. Was he wondering what
Mother thought of the love nest, as he wrongly
supposed it to be?

Catching her smouldering glance, he allowed his
lips to curve in satirical amusement, before his
expression closed up again and the ice-grey eyes
froze her protests once more to silence.

Again he turned to Neil.

'It sounds as if you've made up your mind,'
he said finally. 'Am I to consider you Miss
Maddern's—ah—representative in any discussions
we may have?'

'Fiancé. I'm her fiancé,' Neil objected, so
promptly that Vienna only just stifled a gasp of
surprise.

Brenden Darcour's eyes flicked her like a quick,
cold lash.

'Fiancé,' he drawled, thinning his lips so that his
expression managed to convey instant disbelief. He
stared pointedly at Vienna's ringless fingers before
moving towards the door. 'If you'll give me your
telephone number I'll ring and let you know when
I've finalised arrangements.'

Just when she thought he was leaving, the man
Darcour took several long strides across the room
to the cabinet and the painting; and he stood looking at it, just as Neil had done, for several
moments.

'Very pretty,' he commented, his voice expressionless.

He did not glance at Vienna again, except for a casual inclination of the head as he passed.

It was Neil who ushered him out, once again so carefully creating the impression that he was host. When Neil came back into the room, Vienna asked cautiously, 'Neil, why did you say you were my—that we were engaged?'

'Because we are—of course we are. We've always known it, haven't we? Why do you think I let you go and work for Dr Jason?'

'Why?'

'Because Mother didn't think it wise for me to be getting involved with one of the hospital nursing staff. She considered it inadvisable—you know how people talk.'

'Your mother!'

'We thought it best.' Neil floundered, but not for long. He put his arm around her shoulders and kissed the mutiny from her mouth, and Vienna let herself be persuaded. Because that was what she had been wanting for so long, wasn't it? To be sure of her relationship with Neil, to take the magic step from friendship to something immeasurably deeper, the move towards total commitment ... something she had never wanted to do with any man before him.

Well, now she was taking it ... She felt his arms folded warm around her, his mouth on her mouth, yet the contact wasn't carrying the assurance she expected.

It must be her own fault. Neil's caresses had never before failed to warm and satisfy.

Neil must have felt her misgivings, for he said, 'It's what you want, isn't it, the engagement?'

His voice was aggrieved, and she said yes, it was what she wanted. Because of course it was. If only the man from outback hadn't cheated her by making things happen in this confused way.

When Neil let her go he said, 'I'll talk to Mother, and tomorrow we'll decide what shopping we need to do,' and she said yes again.

It wasn't like her to be so easily led. Vienna had always chosen to think things out, making sure that whatever direction her life went it was by her own design. But something had happened to her resistance tonight. She was being led, and she didn't like it.

After Neil had gone she locked the door, and absentmindedly moved the table from where Neil had placed it close to Brenden Darcour's hand. Then she stood in front of Evelyn Harryn's painting, staring at the isolated homestead in its alien landscape under the red and purple mountains.

She stood there for a long time, just looking, before she went to bed.

CHAPTER TWO

NEXT morning Neil brought her a beautifully-mounted emerald ring. She watched him slip it on to her finger in a confusion of mixed emotions. It was a family heirloom, he told her. It would do for the present, and if she didn't like it they would buy another later. But just now she sensed he was consolidating his position, making it clear to the man with the distant eyes that there was a solid, settled relationship between them, and that he spoke for Vienna.

They bought and packed provisions, and fortunately Neil's big black car was large enough to hold their suitcases of clothing, a car fridge of meat and other perishable food, including a supply of fruit.

Evelyn had spoken about an orchard at Red Vistas, but early November might find most of the fruit unripe, and as the homestead was unoccupied they took sleeping bags and linen and rugs; and the supplies flowed over from the car-trunk to the back seat where Vienna shared space with them.

Neil's mother, Myra, proved to be a delicate-looking, tiny woman whose fragility didn't prevent her claiming the front passenger seat beside her son. She did it firmly, with practised charm.

'You won't mind, Vienna dear, I know. I just can't travel in the rear seat, because of car-sickness. It's really quite awful of me, but I feel you'll understand.'

Vienna said she didn't mind, so she sat alongside a suitcase and two cardboard cartons of groceries and tinned food; and watched the neat, sleek head of Neil's mother beside him in the front seat as they travelled. Myra had beautifully waved silver hair tinted soft mauve, and she wore a draped silk dress in lemon and white, so elegant that Vienna felt over-casual in navy cotton blouse and white flared skirt with a scarlet leather belt clinching her waist, and red-strapped high-heeled shoes. She didn't need the raised eyebrows of Brenden Darcour to tell her the attire was completely un-suitable.

He himself was dressed in yellow and brown checked shirt and slim-legged jeans, and the casual gear accentuated the impression of leashed, con-trolled strength that she had already detected behind the more conventional suit he wore at their first meeting. He drove a large dark-green utility loaded with machinery, its radiator protected by stout black bullbars.

He drove ahead and out of sight once they reached the unsealed road. Sometimes he was a cloud of dust on the horizon, at other times there was nothing to suggest he was anywhere around at all; but Vienna had to admit that his presence, however elusive, made her feel a little less nervous.

Neil had decreed that travelling the whole jour-ney in one day would be too tiring for his mother, so they were booked into a roadside hotel for the first night. The man Darcour wasn't too pleased about that, but Neil insisted.

While they travelled on the bitumen Vienna felt no real misgivings at all, but once they moved off the sealed road and on to the dusty highway that didn't look all that much like a highway at all, she became aware of a hollow sense of foreboding.

Once, Myra said slyly, 'That was a strange thing

for that woman to do, wasn't it? I mean, leaving you all her belongings. Didn't she have any family?'

Myra's eyes were bright with questions, but Vienna said shortly, no, there had been nobody ... She didn't want to talk about Evelyn's loneliness. Evelyn had been fiercely proud. While other patients had visitors, she had sheltered behind books and magazines. She had never lost her independence.

Not one visitor, not a phone call, linked her to the outside world, but she had resisted even the suspicion of sympathy, until one night Vienna found her lying in bed, long after the other patients slept, her face wet with silent tears.

Impulsively, Vienna had curled her hand around the older woman's fingers and held them. Later, somehow, she found herself with arms clasped around shaking shoulders. And afterwards there had been a closeness between them, a contact that flashed in Evelyn's welcoming smile, an eagerness in her voice, whenever Vienna appeared.

After Vienna left the hospital to do the 'specialling' work for Dr Jason, she found herself visiting Evelyn whenever she called to see Neil. It was little enough to offer, although Vienna had always been careful not to become emotionally involved with patients. She knew the rules: a certain amount of detachment made one a better nurse. She'd dinned the advice into juniors often enough.

But something about the proud lonely woman touched her feelings and evoked a response, until she found herself stopping for quiet talks, admiring the painting, listening to stories about the homestead and the outback.

There had been a magnificent garden at Red

Vistas, Evelyn confided. She talked about it wist-fully—oleander and hibiscus and wild purple bou-gainvillaea sprawling in great splashes of colour behind windbreaks. And between the homestead and the rocky mountain range behind it was an orchard and vegetable garden that she described in loving detail.

Vienna had been astonished to learn one day that the old lady had never seen the homestead.

'Red Vistas was my mother's home,' she confes-sed half apologetically, 'when she was a young girl.'

That had been before Evelyn's mother ran away with an itinerant stockman who worked a while on Red Vistas, finding time to collect its only daughter before he rode on to other plains and stony moun-tains, over red or brown or apricot sand, where his wandering feet took him to other jobs on other sheep and cattle stations; and there had been no communication between the owners of Red Vistas and their errant child. The Darcours had been af-fronted by their daughter's careless choosing of a husband: they had been offended by her silence. They closed their home and their hearts, and she insisted defiantly that she really couldn't care.

But the painting of Red Vistas by her father, Ralph, Evelyn's mother had carried always with her.

While other children grew up listening to tales of giants' castles and princely palaces, Evelyn's childhood had been made magical by enchanting stories woven about the homestead and its vivid, vibrant countryside. For Evelyn it had been a dream ... to see one day the long homestead among the red land and the saltbush, the mulga and sprawling gumtrees, with the bold hills like a protective wall behind it.

Sometimes she lay watching the picture, lost in reverie. And once she had said simply to Vienna, 'I can see you there, you know. Wouldn't it be wonderful if you could visit it one day, if you could look inside that beautiful house?'

And Vienna had laughed and shaken her head.

'Not much chance of that.'

'I can see you there,' Evelyn had repeated gently, and Vienna had laughed again.

Now here she was, watching the dust-swirls flung up behind Brenden Darcour's utility far ahead, on her way to visit the place of Evelyn's dreaming.

She sighed, and Myra half twisted again in her seat, her eyes shrewd and assessing as she studied Vienna's flushed cheeks.

'I suppose this will be a valuable property we're going to see. She must have taken a real fancy to you, that old lady.'

Vienna said through stiff lips, 'You might say that.' Because there was no way Myra could understand how she felt about Evelyn.

The road grew more uneven, and Myra lapsed into silence; and several times in the driving mirror Vienna caught Neil's expression, and each time he was frowning.

Although it was spring, the countryside showed only scattered patches of green. The scenery was often barren, not at all enchanting to look at.

Once Myra said wistfully, 'It will probably be much nicer at our overnight stop,' but it wasn't. The hotel proved to be a solitary building set back from the highway not far from a waterhole; a combination petrol station, general store and hotel.

Brenden Darcour waited for them, his heavily-loaded utility parked outside; and when they got out of the comfort of Neil's car and struggled through the heat into the building, Vienna wasn't at all surprised to find the accommodation limited.

'You two ladies won't mind sharing a room, will you?' The owner's wife was friendly and anxious to please, and Vienna said no, they wouldn't mind. But she did mind. She wanted to creep away into a quiet corner and catch up with her chaotic thoughts, which kept presenting her with the ghastly picture of what she was doing; far from home and travelling even farther, with Neil and his mother gently manipulating her into a family arrangement that somehow had begun to appeal less than she had expected.

I must be mad, she told herself. After all the anxious hours—no, months—she had spent fretting because Neil let her leave the hospital without showing he cared for anything more than casual friendship. All the grieving and distress, she thought, bewildered, and now I'm not sure whether I care at all.

The man from outback joined them for the evening meal, and when it was over they sat on an ancient wooden verandah watching the stars. There was no long, slow twilight. Night dropped quickly, as though a shade had been drawn, and suddenly stars shone bright and clear, glittering like early-morning dewdrops in garden spiderwebs.

Vienna half-smiled at her flight of fancy, then she caught the shrewd grey eyes of the outback man watching, almost as if she had spoken her thought aloud.

He and Neil each had a small single room off the verandah, and it was he who suggested retiring

early because they were to continue driving at
dawn, after a quick breakfast. Myra began to protest, but when he added that they ought to reach
Kenora Station by lunchtime tomorrow, and break
the journey there for a meal, she made no further
objection, and allowed Neil to escort her inside.

When Neil and his mother disappeared along the
passageway Vienna stood up quickly, and because
the travelling had made her unsteady she stumbled
on the slender high heels of her red shoes.

Brenden Darcour put out his hand and steadied
her. He held her no longer than he had to, and his
touch was carefully impersonal.

'Don't you have any more sensible footwear than
those?'

'Yes, I do,' she snapped. 'But I'm not going to
unpack my cases tonight.'

His voice was chilly. 'What are you snarling for,
Nursie? Too bad you couldn't share a room with
your beloved. I hope it hasn't upset you too much.
Surely you don't object to sharing with mother?
Just think how well you'll get to know one an-
other.'

Vienna stared at him furiously. There was no
light where they stood, the nearest lamp shone a
small distance away to lure mosquitoes and the
night's other small winged creatures away from the
verandah. Its orange glow cast strange planes of
light and darkness across the rugged face of the
tall man, making mystery of his expression, but
she knew he was laughing at her.

She tried to parry his confidence with her own
strength. It was a little difficult, because he was so
much taller than she was, but she managed it. She
tilted her chin and stared at him defiantly.

'I could have done worse, couldn't I?' she asked

sweetly. 'I mean, I might have had to share a room with you.'

Too late, she would have given anything to call back the words. Her wayward tongue, loosened by tiredness and confusion, had betrayed her. She felt herself flushing scarlet, and knew the man detected her confusion, even in the dark, as he stared down at her out of those cold, chilling eyes.

He could have said so many things. Like, 'No way, lady. I'd sooner sleep in a horse paddock or up a tree,' or any one of a hundred other insults that must have crowded into his mind. But he just stood there in the doorway, so close she could feel his breathing, and his silent contempt came down over her like a blanket.

Tears of anger and embarrassment and weariness filled her eyes, and she felt the betraying tremble of her lips as she turned away from him and marched, head held high, along the passage towards the room she shared with Myra.

She didn't hear him move. He might still be standing there silent in the doorway, and the knowledge kept her from bringing up a hand to wipe away the tears that squeezed from under her eyelashes. He mustn't know how upset she was; she wouldn't give him that satisfaction.

Because she was distressed, she marched past her room and into the bathroom at the end of the passage. She splashed her face with water and smoothed her hair, and when she emerged a few minutes later there was nobody around at all.

She found Myra in the bedroom, covering her immaculate hair with a pink shower cap before she ventured out to the bathroom. It seemed to her that the look Myra offered her was tentative,

questioning. She wasn't all that sure of herself after
all, not in this situation.

She didn't really want to come any more than I
did, Vienna told herself. She's here because she
cares about Neil. Like I do, she added hastily,
before her treacherous feelings surprised her with
more doubts.

Breakfast next morning was a hasty affair, eaten
just before sun-up. Around the waterhole, as the
sun rose, colourful wild birds drank and splashed
and squabbled. A flock of galahs made rose pink
and grey spirals in the sky before settling in an
ancient tree. Later, when the cars started up, the
galahs rose in a wild flurry of wings, screeching;
and that was the last thing Vienna saw as they
drove away along the corrugated road—the pink
and grey spiral in the sky as the birds wheeled
before re-settling themselves in the tree.

Brenden Darcour had warned Neil to travel
slowly, especially over the cattle grids that crossed
the highway.

Neil muttered, 'Just what I need, cattle grids to
lumber over!' and that seemed to set the mood for
the morning.

At midday, they left the highway for an even
less comfortable dirt road, sandy and ridged and
windblown. There were fences with gates to open.
Brenden Darcour drove well ahead, opening and
shutting his own gates, and they followed the
waving plume of his dust.

He had been right about the red shoes being
useless. As Vienna alighted to open and shut the
sixth gate, she silently cursed him for being right.
Her white skirt was impregnated with coloured
dust and so was her hair. She'd been sensible
enough to carry a navy cotton sunhat with shady

brim, but it didn't stop the infiltration of powdery dust. She even breathed it.

At any other time, Vienna might have been delighted with Kenora homestead and its gardens, sheltered behind a stone windbreak and a line of trees; but today she was conscious of her bedraggled appearance and plagued with misgivings.

Melly Taeger, the manager's wife, welcomed them with a delicious meal. Her husband, she explained, was out checking fences. She offered them cool drinks and refreshing showers, and Vienna was astonished to find after coming out from her shower that Bren Darcour sat in the office with her, going over papers and accounts. Neither of them paid her any attention as she passed. Despite her friendliness there was a curious reticence about Melly Taeger, as though she and Bren Darcour shared a secret knowledge. It was natural, Vienna supposed uncomfortably. Those two belonged, they were outback people, while she and Myra and Neil were city intruders. And what was more, she reminded herself not without embarrassment, they shouldn't be here at all.

Subdued, she unlocked her suitcase and changed into fawn cotton slacks with her navy shirt, and a pair of comfortable walking shoes.

An ironic lift of the eyebrows showed that Brenden Darcour noted the change, but he spoke very little as they prepared to drive off again.

The afternoon heat was oppressive, but he said they must stay no longer if they wanted to reach Red Vistas in time to settle in before nightfall.

'Are you staying with us, Mr Darcour?' Myra asked him archly, but he shook his head. He would be driving on to Glenister Two, his own cattle station farther north, he said. He was anxious to get there with his load of machinery.

Vienna was astonished to find herself wishing he could have stayed with them for that first night. He was arrogant and objectionable, and she knew he disliked her for what he thought she was, and perhaps he was right at that, since he had a habit of being right. But his leaving would be like the removal of a support she could have done with for a little longer.

The vast red land both enchanted and frightened her. Never had she seen the air so clear, with trees and rocks on distant hillsides standing out so clear and bright they could have been only a few miles away, instead of in the far distance.

It was the distance that undermined her confidence, the vast stretches of landscape that seemed in some places to go on for ever. But the man from outback would travel with them as far as the homestead, and for that they must be grateful.

When they turned off the highway once more, on to a rough sandy access road that was really nothing but a pair of wheeltracks among clumps of spinifex and grasses, with straggly trees, Vienna found with sinking heart that there were no gates to open and shut. Fences sagged, or had disappeared altogether. Neil said grimly, 'Doesn't look too well cared for, does it?' His enthusiasm was waning.

Myra said nothing, and Vienna once again had the distinct impression that she was here only to do her duty, to make certain her beloved son didn't become engulfed in a situation that might not be to his advantage.

And then, at last, a gate to be opened and shut. Brenden Darcour hadn't waited for them. His utility puffed up red dust well ahead, and disappeared.

Vienna staggered from Neil's car and dragged open the gate. It sagged badly, but at least it was a gate, and the fence still stood, a sign that something had been done to protect Red Vistas from the encroaching environment.

Vienna shook more dust from her clothes and hair as Neil's passing car churned up another cloud to drift over her; and after she closed the gate she saw with horror that the vehicle Neil took such pride in was no longer shining black. It was caked in thick dust and badly streaked where a patch of mulga scrub had brushed and scratched it.

They sat silently for the final part of the journey, until the car bumped across the foothills of a range of mountains that looked like nothing more than great heaps of rock tumbled together, as though it might have been a gigantic rock-dump discarded by the rest of the world out here in the middle of nowhere. The few dispirited green things that clung to its sides hung limp and listless in the heat.

Nobody spoke. Not until they rounded the end of the foothills, and there in a saucer-shaped hollow below them sat the Red Vistas homestead with a few ancient buildings around it and a silver-grey windmill creaking and groaning in the dismal silence.

Neil muttered, 'Oh, my God!' and his mother wailed something incoherent, while Vienna heard her own voice chanting in disbelief, over and over, 'Oh no, oh no!' as if there were no other words she could say.

Because the homestead was derelict. A ghost house, inhabited only by wind and debris and a few pieces of fallen rubble. Unroofed, the stone walls stood firm enough, but inner walls and ceilings, exposed to wind and weather, had collapsed. The

homestead was an empty, crumbling shell, with
verandah posts leaning in crazy disarray like drun-
ken roisterers clinging desperately to the nearest
support in order to remain upright. One or two of
the surrounding buildings appeared intact, but the
gardens of Evelyn Harryn's dreaming had long
gone. A few ghost gums lifted white trunks and
arms along one side of the house; a straggling
windbreak of native trees sagged nearly as badly as
the verandah posts they had once protected.

Neil's foot went down angrily on the accelerator,
and they lurched down the bumpy slope in a clatter
of rattling stones and rising dust.

Perhaps it was disappointment that made Neil
careless, or perhaps dust obscured his view, because
the car came to a stop between two jagged boulders, clipping the edge of one so that it spun the
car around in an uncontrolled semi-circle. Because
Neil didn't stop quickly enough, the car came to
rest against the second boulder with a crunch that
buckled bodywork and jammed it hard over the
front wheel.

It all happened quite gently, they were almost
stationary, and seat-belts protected them from
injury. But there was thunder in Neil's face as he
surveyed the damage, and Vienna climbed out from
under cartons of groceries, aware of a simmering
of hysterical laughter somewhere beneath stress
and disappointment. Resolutely she clamped it
back. Hysteria was out.

The utility had disappeared over a distant rise.
Now Brenden Darcour drove back from wherever
he had been and pulled up some way from Neil's
car. Face carefully impassive, the man from outback approached. After one quick look at Vienna,
he turned his attention to the damaged car.

It was Myra who broke the silence. Tight-lipped and pale, but with will and dignity unimpaired, she accosted the tall man.

'Mr Darcour, I find it inexplicable that you should have allowed us to be brought into this—this—wilderness, without a word of warning. You must have known——'

Neil interrupted stiffly, 'I take it you were aware of the condition of this homestead?'

The man remained unflappable, his grey eyes steady and steel-cold.

'I was aware of it.'

Myra's eyes flashed. 'How could you allow us to undertake this arduous journey——'

He did not quail before her righteous indignation.

'You wanted to see the outback,' he reminded her gently. 'The shearers' quarters are quite habitable—they're used regularly by drovers. There's a kitchen, plenty of water, and an excellent stove.' He spoke directly to Neil. 'You won't have any trouble finding dry wood for the stove. There's plenty of it about.'

Again Vienna felt the bubble of wild, wild laughter. Again she managed to smother it.

Neil said stiffly, 'Of course, we'll go straight back. Immediately.'

'In that car? You'll have some repairs to do first. You won't be able to move it as it is.'

'Well, can't you help?' Neil's control was snapping. 'You must be able to do something.'

'I can get back here with my overseer tomorrow. He's a mechanic. It'll take a bit of hammering to get that bodywork away from the wheel and you could have damaged the axle. I'm sorry I can't stay with you tonight, but I have visitors arriving at

Glenister Two this afternoon in the mail plane, and this machinery is needed urgently. You'll be all right here, the old shearers' quarters are still comfortable.'

'The shearers' quarters?' Myra uttered faintly. She looked with disbelief at Brenden Darcour as he stood, unperturbed, leaning against one of the boulders beside the trapped car. 'You must be able to do something!' she almost begged.

'Not tonight.' He shook his head briefly. 'There's nothing to worry about. You shouldn't strike any trouble, but if you do my drovers are camped not far away.' He gave Myra a perfunctory smile. 'I've told them you're here. All you have to do is settle in as quickly as you can. And if you don't get started,' he pointed out reasonably, 'it could get dark before you're organised.'

'And what do we do for lighting?'

'Didn't you bring a gas-lamp or torches?' He swung over to his vehicle, and came back bearing a heavy flashlight. 'You didn't come very well equipped.' He cast a sceptical glance at Neil. 'Did you bring milk? Fruit? Bread?'

'Yes, we did.' Neil's temper was running short. He looked nervous, running his fingers through usually immaculate dark hair. He was hot, tired and distressed, as they all were, all except the man from Glenister Two, who was evidently as much accustomed to heat as he was to distance. He remained outwardly calm and unaffected, a little terse, naturally, but obviously unmoved by the fact that he had deliberately let them arrive at a deserted homestead.

He said, 'There's a dried-out claypan south of the homestead, we use it sometimes as a landing strip. I may have to fly down tomorrow, if time is short. We'll fix your car, and meanwhile I'll contact Kenora tonight and tell them you may call in for a meal on your way home. Think you could find your way back there?'

Neil said huffily, 'Of course,' but Myra showed signs of nervousness at Brenden Darcour's departure.

She ventured, 'Couldn't you, Mr—er—couldn't you send for help tonight?'

'I'll bring it,' he answered politely, 'some time tomorrow, without fail. Meanwhile, you *do* have matches? For the stove——'

'A wood fire stove!' Myra's voice was fainter than ever. 'I really don't know—Vienna will have to——'

He smiled suddenly, a satirical smile that had no kindness in it at all.

'Of course,' he agreed softly. 'Miss Maddern will have to, won't she? But then I'm sure she's perfectly capable.'

Vienna said suddenly, 'If this homestead is deserted, whose animals are those under the trees?'

The man's face grew suddenly sharper.

'Those *cattle*,' he amended levelly, 'are mine.'

'On *my* land?'

'On *our* land.'

She stared at him in disbelief. 'You mean you're—you're the other person? You own the other half of Red Vistas?'

His eyebrows lifted haughtily, as if to rebuke her astonishment.

'Naturally,' he said. 'For what it's worth. Why else would I be foolish enough to offer money for a share of worthless land?'

Neil demanded crossly, 'If it's yours, why don't

you keep it in better order? Its condition is a disgrace!'

The man's face was grim.

'Because it's not worth keeping in order. Red Vistas land has been useless for years. It's fit for nothing but a stop-over. Old man Darcour became a recluse after his wife died, and his son was equally useless. They finished up retreating to the city, and the latest Darcour put in a manager. The manager was an idiot. He overstocked the land to make quick profits. He ran sheep as well as cattle, and far too many of each. Of course, he killed the land. Once the herbage goes, there's nothing to hold the soil together. It blows away with every puff of wind. This country has a way of dealing with avarice, and it dealt pretty speedily with that bloke.'

'Then why are your cattle here?' Vienna challenged.

'They're passing through, on their way to Kenora for the sales. That's all this land is good for now, probably all it ever will be good for. Most of it's beyond reclaiming—thanks to one man's neglect and another man's greed.'

Vienna moved uncomfortably. Those grey eyes, so used to scanning long distances, were very good at probing close-up. She thought she knew exactly what the man was thinking. This land has a way of dealing with avarice, he had stated; and if the comment was slanted, then it could have been aimed directly at her.

One man's greed . . . no doubt he applied those words to today as well as yesterday. She knew and he knew that only by accident had she become in any way the possible part-owner of Red Vistas. But for an old lady's whim she would never have owned the enchanting painting, let alone the derelict reality. The greedy, he was saying to her, get exactly what they deserve. Nothing . . .

How it must have amused him, she thought bitterly, to lead them here, to the desolation that had once been Red Vistas.

Myra wailed, 'But you can't leave us here without protection!' and the man Darcour took his disparaging gaze away from Vienna. For all his apparent calm, his voice was impatient, a little throaty.

'Look, I still have two or three hours' driving ahead of me, including some night driving. You're all right here providing you're sensible and don't go straying off looking for snakes in the hot sun tomorrow morning. If you need help, my drovers are camped at the next waterhole, half a mile away. They'll move on early in the morning, but if you want anything let them know before they leave. They know you're here.'

Myra echoed faintly, 'Snakes!' and the merest glimmer of amusement flickered in his eyes.

'You'll have no worries, Mrs Rensome. You've a trained nurse with you, don't forget.'

Vienna shot him a smouldering look.

He went on calmly, 'The water is safe to use. Boil it first, if you like, but what's in the tank is good clear water. I'll be here tomorrow, as soon as I can make it.'

Vienna asked awkwardly, 'Do you want a cup of tea before you leave?' and his teeth flashed in an unexpected smile.

'No, thank you, Nurse. I won't wait.'

Of course he wouldn't wait, and he wasn't wasting words, either. They had wrecked his day. His drovers must sleep under the stars instead of in the shearers quarters, as they usually did. He would travel on, probably in the darkness, without his flashlight. No wonder he was anxious to be off. She didn't blame him.

Vienna had a torch somewhere in the car. She rummaged until she found it, while he stood with Neil making a last-minute check of their provisions. He was on his way back to his utility when she unearthed her small torch, and ran after him.

'Here,' she said, 'you'd better take this. It's not much, but it's better than nothing, and you may need it.'

'Very considerate.' His lips curled. Now she was looking at him across the wall of hostility again. She said crossly,

'It isn't considerate. I don't like you. But I don't want to be responsible if you have a breakdown in the dark and we're using your flashlight, so here you are.'

She held it out belligerently, and he took it from her slowly, thoughtfully, surveying her from under those ironic eyebrows.

'So you don't like me?'

'No, I don't.' She scowled at him. 'I know what you—what you probably think about me; but that's no excuse for bringing us to a place like this. That was a rotten thing to do,' she flashed, 'leaving Myra in this tumbledown house. You knew she'd hate it.' She caught his sardonic glance, and her voice wavered. 'You didn't have to take out your spite on—on a defenceless person——'

He flicked her with an ironic glance.

'Your future mother-in-law, Sister Maddern, is about as defenceless as a funnelweb spider.'

But he had softened. Those penetrating grey eyes took in her dishevelled appearance, noticed the dust stains and the weariness, and the droop of tired lips as she faced him defiantly.

Vienna was travel-stained, and more than that, bitterly disillusioned. It wasn't that she desired to own any part of Red Vistas, but she had needed to know that it was there. All those months Evelyn had lain in bed, easing her pain by dreaming of the beautiful homestead and its gardens, while it had been crumbling away, fruit trees withering, flowers burning in the sun and wind, until there was nothing left that even remotely resembled the picture. Her painting was a delusion.

She looked back now, over her shoulder at the reality, with bitterness. Brenden Darcour seemed to read her thoughts.

'Not quite up to expectations, Sister Maddern?' She must be really tired, because she couldn't stop the tears that were pushing at her eyes; but she challenged him through their gleaming.

'I don't care. I'm glad she didn't see it.' He seemed to know what she meant . . . that Evelyn Harryn had died believing in an enchantment that had been destroyed long ago, if indeed it had ever existed exactly as Ralph Darcour had pictured it.

Bren Darcour stroked his lower lip with one strong thumb and watched her carefully. When he did speak his voice was very careful, very bland.

'Hadn't you better stop dramatising and get to work?' He nodded to where Neil was begrudgingly carrying cases into the shearers' hut.

She asked, trying not to sound anxious, 'I suppose you really *do* intend coming back tomorrow?'

He replied calmly, 'I'll be here tomorrow some time, you can rely on that. Wings or wheels.'

'Wings or——? Oh, you mean you might fly or you might drive?'

His lips twitched. 'Very bright, Nursie.' He was making her feel selfconscious and she hated him

for it. To her surprise he dropped the torch on to
the seat of his utility but did not climb in after it.
Instead, he reached out and cupped one strong
brown hand under her chin, curving his fingers
around her throat, his thumb fitting neatly into
the cleft of her chin, so that she was imprisoned.

'Green eyes, black hair—a dangerous combination. You could have been called for a witch a few
centuries ago. Did you know that?'

She wouldn't answer him. It took all her will-
power not to pull away from those searching
eyes . . .

'You've a sprinkling of freckles on your cheeks
already, Nurse. Very becoming. But let it be a
warning to you—no wandering around in the hot
sun tomorrow, even with a hat on. You'd better
tell the others. I don't want to find a couple of
sunstroke cases on my hands when I get back here
tomorrow.'

Vienna tilted her chin. 'I can assure you, Mr
Darcour, neither my complexion nor I are half as
fragile as you might like to think.'

'That's good.' But he said it absently, as if he
might already have other things on his mind. He
took his hand away from her throat, then said
calmly, 'As a matter of fact, things haven't
happened exactly the way I planned. My intention
was to give your calculating boy-friend a hell of a
shock, then let you all follow me and spend a few
days at Glenister Two, since you were so anxious
to see the outback. But I didn't allow for your boy-
friend smashing his car. Clumsy, isn't he?' When
she didn't answer he went on, 'My ute is heavily
loaded already. I can't take you all with me. So
here you must stay for a few more hours, among
the—er—ruins of Pompeii.'

Vienna said scathingly, 'You could have told us about those ruins, don't you think?' And his eyes were suddenly cold steel.

'Do you really think that would have stopped your boy-friend, Nursie?' While she stared at him, searching for words, he added relentlessly, 'I'll answer that question for you. He wouldn't have believed it, not for a minute.' His smile was bleak and unpleasant. 'He'd have put me down for a smooth-talking liar. And so would you,' he added softly. 'Wouldn't you, Nursie? Don't you think you'd better be truthful and admit it?'

Perhaps. Perhaps not. She couldn't be really sure even now, whether she would have accepted his word, but she thought she might have believed him.

He watched her changing expression with shrewd eyes.

'I told you, the shearers' quarters are comfortable enough, just for one night,' he drawled, and when she looked back at them doubtfully, he added soft-voiced, 'You could do a lot worse, couldn't you?'

So he remembered! That was what she had said to him at the hotel. 'I could do a lot worse, I might have had to share with you . . .' He had saved it up and served it back to her now.

'So how about rustling up your two charges a meal, before the dark comes down, and organising a good sleep for everybody.'

He wouldn't get a good night's sleep. Not by the time he arrived at Glenister Two in darkness, unloaded his machinery, welcomed his visitors, and made plans to come back here tomorrow.

He was glancing past her, at the sand-drifts and the stunted trees. 'Not exactly Adelaide, is it? But it's what you asked for, Sister Maddern.'

She answered him with asperity. 'What you mean is, I should never have left home.'

The austere face lightened a little, the rugged jaw relaxed.

'Oh, I wouldn't say that, Miss Maddern. Not yet, anyway.'

Vienna turned on her heel and marched away, and his mocking laughter followed her. She tried hard not to turn and look back at him as he got into the utility. It took a lot of effort, but she managed it. The big man with the chilly eyes was leaving and she had no logical reason to feel bereft, but that was how she felt. Insecure, because he wasn't going to be near. She heard the utility drive away, and the diminishing sound did something to her confidence.

Not until she reached the car where Neil grumpily unloaded gear did Vienna look back; and by that time the utility was only a wavering plume of dust in the distance. She took a carton of groceries from Neil and carried it to the stone building. Myra sat on a wooden bench outside.

'It's clean in there,' she admitted. 'And there are bunks.' A lot of her assurance had vanished. She looked searchingly at Vienna, and Vienna pulled out her confidence-smile from somewhere deep under misgivings.

Myra said wistfully, 'At least we'll have a roof over our heads.' But her eyelids flickered as she glanced towards the homestead with its dust drifts and toppled verandah-posts, and she blinked apologetically at Vienna as if she, too, might have been feeling daunted.

Vienna hesitated in the doorway. 'Maybe,' she suggested gently, 'you could organise the sleeping-bags—that's if you feel like it. I'll get a meal so we'll settle in before dark. He's—Mr Darcour—he's coming for us tomorrow.'

'I hope so.' Myra looked around her at the distance, clarified by the clear light of outback, so that it seemed the whole planet might have stretched before her. She shivered slightly, and looked again at Vienna.

'There's so much space. I've never seen so much of the earth at one time. We shouldn't have come, should we?'

Vienna insisted stoutly, 'Of course we should.' She hoped she'd convinced Myra; she knew with a flash of honesty that she had come nowhere near convincing herself.

After a meal they watched the sunset, a swift and brilliant splashing of colour poured over the landscape before darkness fell. They could not hear sounds from the drovers' camp. There was only one sign of life ... high above the mountains at the back of the homestead, an eagle glided against a backdrop of crimson cloud. He hovered smoothly and easily, making scarcely any wing-movements at all, floating high and free, black and watchful, until the darkness fell.

Myra spoke suddenly, uneasily. 'That Mr Darcour—he promised? To come back here, I mean?'

Vienna smiled with determined confidence.

'Yes,' she said, 'he promised.'

She hoped she was right. Surely he wouldn't leave them here, in the middle of nowhere, for more than one night. He *had* promised, hadn't he?

Later, as they lay in their sleeping-bags, each of them in a small separate room that Myra likened shudderingly to a 'prison cell', Vienna looked out through the rectangle of wired window space, and found herself childishly clinging to that promise.

'Wings or wheels,' he had said. She didn't care which, so long as he came; and that was quite ridiculous really, because she disliked him and his discerning grey eyes intensely. Yet his power aura did something to bolster her confidence. He supported while he threatened.

She knew he didn't like her, by the ironic twist of that hard mouth, the cool distant voice, not rough or crude like she might have expected of an outback man, but all the more menacing because of its complete control . . . as though he judged her and found her contemptible. And because she saw his point of view so clearly—that she had latched on to a weak and credulous old lady, and was grasping for what she could get—because of that, she wondered whether she was reading more condemnation into the bitter voice than its owner intended.

It had been weak of her to let Neil pressure her into coming. She couldn't understand her own behaviour. Nothing would persuade her to accept either money or a share in the property. So why was she here, following the stranger—together with Neil who was rapidly becoming another stranger—into a predicament she could well do without?

'We shouldn't have come.' Vienna found herself echoing Myra's words as she fell asleep.

CHAPTER THREE

THE drovers left early next morning. Vienna heard the distant barking of dogs, the crack of stock-whips. They sounded a long way off, and they were going even farther.

She crawled out of her sleeping-bag and pulled on slacks and a coloured shirt of handprinted cotton with pictures of coral islands and palm trees printed all over it. It didn't seem entirely suitable, but it was long-sleeved and cool, and she had to be ready for heat when the sun came up.

She tiptoed quietly outside. Her hair needed washing, and all their dusty clothes lay in a heap beside a blue plastic bucket, where she had collec-ted them last night. She found soap and shampoo and made her way with bucket and clothes to the waterhole.

The cattle had disappeared, but there were movements in the pre-dawn shadows around the water. Vienna looked doubtfully at the soap in her hand. She had probably better not use it and pol-lute the waterhole . . . she filled the bucket and made a slaphappy job of shampooing her hair, then she washed the dusty clothes, being careful to throw the soapy water where it was swallowed up by sand. After that, she hung the wet gear on the branches of a dead tree to dry in the wind.

Before she left, the bright birds of the wild places came down to drink at the waterhole, disturbing the daybreak with shrill voices. They hardly seemed to notice her at all. There were white corellas with

yellow underwings, a flock of tiny green budg-
erigars, and other birds she did not recognise.

The wind increased and an ancient gumtree
shook its leaves, while puffs of swirling sand blew
about. Vienna looked at her flapping clothes, and
sighed. Goodness knows, she thought despond-
ently, how much dust they'll collect while they're
hanging there. But as she walked towards the stone
building where Neil and his mother still slept, the
sun rose clear of the horizon and she watched
delighted as it daubed yellow and purple and
scarlet splashes everywhere. The mulga turned
silver; the spinifex raw gold; and on the rocky hills
daybreak threw temporary smudges of indigo and
scarlet.

Later, after they had breakfasted, Vienna shook
dust out of her newly-washed clothing, and tried
to recapture the magic of that sunrise. She might
never see another extravagance of light like that.
But already most of it was gone. The climbing sun
returned every landmark to its original shape and
colour and texture, and she could not recapture in
her memory the swift, dramatic colour changes of
the sunrise.

Neil fussed over the car. He seemed to think the
accident was her fault. Myra said very little.

Neil, away from the polished desk and all the
trappings of authority, seemed somehow to lose
stature. His usually smooth dark hair fell forward
on to a flushed forehead as he muttered abuse at
the crumpled bodywork, the crushing rock. Vienna
sighed and went inside to gather up the sleeping-
bags. They must have everything ready for the man
from Glenister Two when he arrived. She appreciated that his time was valuable and already he
had wasted enough of it on them. He mightn't be

too agreeable after the long drive and the short night's sleep.

Maybe he would want lunch. She set about planning what they would eat, looking around the shearers' kitchen for cooking utensils. The drovers must be using it regularly, because the sand that lay in heaps through all the rooms of the derelict homestead had not been allowed to gather here. Accommodation was rough but reasonable, water plentiful, and the stove presented no problems.

Vienna tied her black hair into two ponytails, and fastened them with white ribbon, then she put on the navy sunhat and went outside, ready to gather wood.

On the bench, Myra sat halfheartedly brushing dust out of her hair. She wasn't making a very good job of it, probably because she was used to a hairdresser, and with a flash of sympathy Vienna helped brush and set the mauve-tinted silver waves to something like their original beauty. Then she went looking for wood.

When the stove was lit she put on a large pot of beef and orange stew, using the meat they had brought with them and a generous supply of potatoes and carrots and onions as well as the flavouring oranges and rind; because the man from Glenister Two would be hungry.

But it was mid-afternoon before Brenden Darcour arrived. They had eaten lunch and cleared away, and packed everything in readiness; and because it was probably the last chance she would ever have, Vienna wandered over to the wrecked homestead, moving in the protection of its walls while she tried to imagine the rooms and the gardens as they once might have been. She was exploring the sand-patch that had once been a kit-

chen garden when she heard the distant drone of
the plane; and because she had discovered among
the sand drifts a twisted piece of sage with purple
buds, she did not hurry to the claypan to see the
landing. But she did look up, and it seemed to her
somehow appropriate that the small plane banked
and glided over the rugged mountains behind Red
Vistas just where the eagle had soared in the red
sky of yesterday's sunset.

Vienna went back to digging out the root of sage.
Evelyn had talked about a herb garden, and this
must be all that remained; and for some reason
it seemed important to Vienna that she capture
this last remnant of Evelyn's broken dreaming.
Fanciful, perhaps, but she dug her hands into the
sand, scraping it away and feeling for roots among
the grit. She was still probing when the shadow fell
across her hands, and she looked up to see the man
from Glenister Two watching her grimly.

'Leave it, Miss Maddern.' His voice was terse.
'There won't be another garden here, not for a long
time, if ever.'

'Why not? There's water——'

'Water isn't the problem. Everything has turned
to dust, there's nothing left for roots to hold on to.
The first good breeze will blow your plant away.'

Vienna scooped the last of the choking sand
away from the stringy root of sage, and held it in
her hand.

'May I take it?'

His mouth twisted. 'I thought you probably
considered it yours.'

The voice mocked her, and she found herself
hesitating. It would be splendid to make a defiant
gesture, to hurl the sage down among the dust, but
something stopped her.

'Oh, take the damned thing!' He pushed her roughly ahead of him.

Vienna offered with stilted politeness, 'Will you have something to eat? Sandwiches, or a cup of tea? I have a thermos.'

'No, thank you. I've just been explaining to your friends that my mechanic is busy, so I'll fly you all back with me to Glenister Two. You'll get your outback holiday after all, and Terry will drive down and fix your car as soon as he's free.'

Vienna protested uneasily, 'We've inconvenienced you enough. Surely there must be some other way?'

But his smile was not encouraging.

'If there were any other way, Miss Maddern, don't you think I might have used it?'

He walked behind her, perilously close, Vienna thought. To her annoyance she found herself so aware of him that she hurried, like a child trying to get away from authority—like a lost maiden, with the dragon breathing down her neck.

Stop it, she told herself, and it was then she stumbled, tripping on a piece of rubble hidden in the sand. She got to her feet so fast it seemed like one movement, the falling and the rising, yet he was there before her. His hand closed around her elbow. His keen eyes searched her face for signs of pain, finding none.

He picked up her hat, and she took it and pulled it down low on her forehead, the piece of sage still clutched childishly in her hand, her fingers closed around it in a hard fist.

He said, his voice mild, 'Washed your hair this morning, did you?'

'Yes, I did. In the waterhole. *And* our clothes. Do you mind?'

He said levelly, 'Not unless you put soap in our water. But then you wouldn't do that, would you?'

His mouth made a hard line. Vienna stood in his way and tilted her chin and glared at him with all the defiance she could muster.

'No, I didn't. I used a bucket, and I threw the soapy water in the sand. You can go and look, if you're all that anxious to find something to complain about. I haven't put one bubble in your precious waterhole.'

I nearly did, she should have admitted. It was only at the last moment she had remembered the birds and animals that drank there, and wondered about polluting the water with soap. But she wouldn't tell him that. She had enough strikes against her, without adding another one.

He said, almost as though his intuition had penetrated her thinking, 'That's one point to you, isn't it, Nursie?'

Probably the only one, Vienna admitted to herself. There wasn't likely to be another. She couldn't imagine herself doing anything else that would earn his pleasure or deflect his wrath. It wasn't going to be that kind of relationship, anybody could see that.

He said no more to her as they collected their belongings and he stowed everything in the tail of the plane. Before they left, Neil's car was covered with a tarpaulin to protect it from weather and flying sand.

It was only when they landed on the airstrip at Glenister Two that Vienna realised just how crumpled and disreputable she appeared, despite her efforts to shake dust out of hair and clothing.

A large four-wheel-drive vehicle—a Range Rover, she discovered as they walked towards it—waited under trees alongside the small airstrip; and beside it lounged one of the most vibrant girls she had ever seen. She wore white shorts and a scarlet skinny-rib top, and all-over suntan covered her in bronze perfection. Her beautiful limbs were smooth and gleaming. She was a living doll, and well she knew it.

Oh, so confident she was, watching them straggle from the plane into the dry-season heat. Oh, so confident and oh, so cool, her hair skilfully cut into a short cap of shining brown, her mouth an extravagance of scarlet. Only her eyes were heartless. A pale and shallow blue like watered silk, they surveyed Vienna with contemptuous lack of interest, then turned full-beam on the man who stacked suitcases into the vehicle as if they weighed nothing at all.

'Bren, how darling of you to fly to the rescue!'

He said, almost as if she had not spoken, 'What happened to Terry?' and she pouted, a frankly sexual and challenging pucker of the lips, lifting her shoulders in a graceful shrug.

'How should I know, darling? He wasn't around, so I took the Range Rover and came to meet you.' She pouted again. 'Aren't you going to thank me?'

The grim face relaxed, then. He said, 'Later, maybe.' But he smiled at her, and the remote grey eyes that Vienna had found so chilling and off-putting, warmed into life as he spoke to her. 'Meanwhile, Luci, meet your fellow guests, then we'll get back to the homestead and cool drinks.'

As they climbed into the Range Rover he asked, almost as an afterthought, 'Where's young Abigail?' and Luci pouted again, this time crossly.

'She wanted to come, but I told her there was no room, so now of course she's sulking. She went off mumbling something about a swim. She really is a most difficult child, Bren.'

Luci managed to work up a flicker of interest in
Neil, but Vienna and Myra she discarded as neg-
ligible. Not a glimmer of friendliness or curosity
showed in her expression. She chatted all the way
to the homestead, her cool superior voice directed
only at the man whom she called darling . . .

Vienna didn't want to be included. As the Range
Rover passed through the homestead gateway,
along a curved gritty driveway behind a row of
windbreaking trees, she saw with a shock of bitterness that Glenister Two was everything Red Vistas
once might have been in the days when Ralph
Darcour painted it. There were creepers with
gold, and white, flowers climbing verandah
posts; and sheltered by overhanging eaves of the
wide verandah, leafless trees of frangipanni wafted
fragrance from early flowers, large and sweetly
perfumed, some creamy-yellow, others tinged
pink.

A little way off, sheltered by scattered trees,
Vienna saw a swimming pool with a small figure
splashing at one end . . . the 'difficult child', no
doubt . . . and behind the pool a strip of rock
garden bright with some variety of daisies with
bold yellow and orange faces. A row of traveller's
palms spread large stiff fans against the sky, and
not far away a trellised summerhouse was covered
in sprawling bougainvillaeas, the vivid bracts
making fragile 'paper-flowers' of purple, magenta,
and deep rose.

In the centre of the vast country, Glenister Two
had created for itself a breathtakingly beautiful
oasis that had little in common with saltbush or
mulga.

Vienna had no doubt that behind the homestead

there flourished an orchard and kitchen garden such as Evelyn Harryn had dreamed about.

'A good man,' Evelyn had asserted confidently, 'can make things grow, anything ... anywhere ... if he wants it enough. If he'll work. That's what my mother always said.'

Numbly Vienna followed the girl Luci across the verandah and into the homestead. A plump, pleasant woman with honey-coloured hair and bright amber eyes welcomed them. She was Dorothy Green, the overseer's wife, and she had come out of the kitchen because she wore a voluminous apron and there were smudges of flour on her hands.

After introductions Bren asked again, 'Where's Terry?'

'He went to have a look at that bore you were worried about. Luci offered to pick you all up at the airstrip.'

He nodded, and helped Neil carry luggage on to the verandah. Dorothy showed them all to their rooms, and as she opened her suitcase to unpack, Vienna realised that Dorothy Green's voice had been the first to offer any warmth of welcome. She felt overwhelmingly grateful. Confidence was getting lower all the time, but Dorothy managed to prevent its complete disappearance.

Vienna pulled a wry face at her dishevelled reflection in the bedside mirror; but after a shower and freshen-up she looked around her appreciatively at the neat room with its flowered curtains and bedspread. On the small bedside table two sprays of frangipanni, one pink and one creamy-yellow, balanced in a white vase. Vienna wondered whose thought it was. She wondered too whether she should offer any help in the kitchen.

Their arrival must have brought added problems
for Dorothy.

She dressed in a slender white crêpe dress, and
brushed her hair to restore its lost shining. The
Darcour man had been right about her freckles.
They lurked under her new honey tan in a light
sprinkling over each cheekbone, but with a little
make-up and a hint of blusher they were almost
obscured. She unearthed her poor twisted sage root
and tucked it into the vase among the flowers. Then
she considered the frangipanni impishly. One of
those exotic flowers would look simply lovely in
her hair; but she wasn't here to look decorative, of
course. They were all here on sufferance, the three
of them.

She sighed, and left the black shining of her hair
unadorned.

Nevertheless when she and Dorothy Green met
in the passage, Dorothy raised her eyebrows in
mock surprise.

'Transformation!' she laughed. 'I didn't realise
there was a beauty hiding under all that dust.'

'Thank you.' Vienna felt herself flushing. 'You're
restoring my morale, even if you do exaggerate.
Can I help you in the kitchen? We must be quite a
burden, three unexpected guests.'

Dorothy shook her head.

'You're to go into the sitting room—boss's
orders. It's the front room, straight ahead past the
bedrooms, at the end of the passage. Cool drinks
are waiting, and I bet you'll be glad of them.' She
looked at Vienna through shrewd but friendly eyes.
'Bit of an ordeal, was it? Bad luck, being stranded
like that.'

Vienna wondered how much Dorothy knew, and
whether she would have been quite so friendly had

she realised exactly how her extra three visitors had come to arrive at Glenister Two.

She was saying now, 'I'll tell you what you might do, if you really don't mind. It would be a tremendous help if you could take over the clearing away afterwards. Including dish-washing, if you're so inclined. If not, leave it for me in the morning.'

'No trouble at all. I'll be glad of something to do.'

'Then I'll go home as soon as the meal is served, and get ready for Terry's evening meal.'

Vienna queried, 'Home?'

'Oh yes. Didn't anybody tell you? My husband is Bren's overseer. We live in a bungalow behind the kitchen garden and through the citrus grove. You'll find us easily enough. Come and have a talk whenever you feel like it—just follow the path past the store.'

'Thank you. I'm sorry we're a nuisance——'

'No nuisance at all.' Her merry eyes were unworried. 'We have two visitors arrived late yesterday, young Abby who's twelve, and her aunt Luci, whom you've already met. They're staying for a week or so. All I have to do is cook a little more of everything, though I would be grateful if you don't mind clearing away. I'll be here to get breakfast tomorrow morning.'

Vienna offered impulsively, 'I'll help you. Maybe I could do it on my own after that, while we're here, and save you coming up if you're busy.'

Dorothy laughed. 'We'll see. We're very early risers here—breakfast before dawn. You could be fast asleep at that hour.'

'I'm a nursing Sister. I work at a geriatric hospital, a private nursing home, so I'm used to odd hours,' Vienna told her.

Dorothy's eyebrows lifted again. 'Are you really? I didn't think you were old enough, if you don't mind a personal comment. I put you down as eighteen or nineteen.'

'I'm twenty-two, nearly twenty-three.'

'Mmm, a very charming twenty-three. All right, I accept your offer with many thanks. I've three youngsters doing schooling by correspondence and School of the Air, so the supervision takes a fair bit of my time. But you must make sure you enjoy your stay, as well as working. There's a lot to see on a cattle run. This your first visit to the outback?'

Vienna nodded. And my last, she added silently to herself, but Dorothy's good humour was so infectious she found herself smiling.

'Don't worry, a little work won't hurt me. It'll keep me on my toes!'

As she went into the large room at the front of the homestead, where everyone else was already gathered, Vienna found herself thinking ruefully, Just as well I didn't wear flowers in my hair. They wouldn't look appropriate at the kitchen sink! Her lips curved in a faint smile, and the man pouring drinks at the bar glanced at her curiously as she came into the room.

He called, 'What will you have to drink, Miss Maddern?'

He was very careful to say Miss Maddern, Vienna noticed, although they were all using first names, and he had during introductions to Luci and Dorothy suggested she might call him Bren.

'Gin and tonic, thank you. If it's available.'

As she walked towards him, he murmured softly, 'We're amusing you?' and the words made a question.

'Not particularly. Why?'

'You were smiling.'

'Oh. Well, I didn't mean to.'

His lips twitched. 'Don't let us stop you, Miss Maddern. Any time you feel amused——'

The girl Luci didn't intend to allow any conversation with the big cattleman that didn't revolve around her. She draped herself against the polished bar, and puckered her mouth provocatively as she held out her empty glass.

'I'm dry, Bren.'

The man's checked shirt had been changed for chocolate brown silk and the tailored beige slacks he wore moulded slim hips and lean diaphragm so that as he moved the body beneath pressed against the clothing. Vienna found herself aware of his movements in a way that disturbed her. This man wore clothes, not as other men wore them, for warmth and comfort or for covering, but with a kind of lazy arrogance, as if he would throw them off at the first opportunity—as though he suffered them for convention's sake, with the lean hard body scarcely concealing its impatience with the trappings of so-called civilisation.

Vienna moved across the room to talk to Neil, and wasn't really surprised to find him not nearly so cordial as he had been before the Red Vistas catastrophe. His dreams of marrying an heiress, Vienna was horrified to discover herself suspecting, had faded; and so had his enthusiasm. She pulled herself up sharply. This was no time to turn cynical, and she wasn't being fair to Neil. He must be hot and tired, as well as disappointed.

Myra had regained most of her poise. Dressed in graceful Italian silk, and back to her usual elegance, she began asking Luci some deftly probing questions about her background and her relationship to the master of Glenister Two; and Vienna saw that Luci answered shortly and with undisguised resentment.

Even when Myra diplomatically managed to bring into the conversation her distant relatives who were 'on the land', Luci remained almost rudely aloof and superior, and not remotely interested in the visitor who had appeared so unexpectedly from nowhere.

Except for Vienna. Luci *was* faintly interested, now that the other girl had scrubbed up into something that looked like competition. Several times Vienna found herself the target of sharp, speculative glances, and because she was growing angry she almost overlooked the young girl who came and stood silently beside her chair, sipping a glass of bitter lemon.

Vienna knew that Abby was twelve years old, because Dorothy had told her so, but the girl standing beside her chair had a strange maturity, a self-contained quietness unusual in someone her age. Her gathered cotton dress was old-fashioned, its long embroidered skirt might have looked appealing on some more vibrant girl, but it was in no way suitable for the mouselike creature who hovered silently at Vienna's elbow. Abby wore it as if she knew how unbecoming it was and didn't really care.

She inspected each of the newcomers with secretive grey eyes, very much like the eyes of her Uncle Bren; but unlike him she had a tiny pointed face, fine auburn hair straggling to her shoulders, and an air of diffidence and suspicion.

Vienna moved her elbow from where it rested on the wide chair-arm.

'Share my seat?'

The girl surveyed her, without smiling, then shrugged her thin shoulders.

'I don't mind if I do.'

Her voice had a clear sweetness, and although she had not smiled, she sat down on the arm of Vienna's chair and stayed there quietly; and when they went in to the evening meal, Vienna found Abby watching her quietly, with little secret glances, until they went back to the sitting room for coffee.

Afterwards, Vienna was filling the enormous kitchen sink with hot water when Abby joined her. Silently, she picked up a tea-towel.

Vienna said gently, 'You don't have to, you know. I expect you're here on holidays, aren't you?'

'Not exactly.' Abby spoke gruffly this time. 'And I might as well help.' But as she wiped plates and stacked them in the racks, she became more talkative. 'There isn't anything to do out there, anyway,' she confided. 'Uncle Bren's gone to his office, and Aunt Luci is playing records and making up to your boy-friend.' She looked at Vienna with calm, candid eyes. 'She's only filling in time, though. It's Uncle Bren she's after. He's her main target. It's him she really wants.'

Vienna said coldly, 'That doesn't sound very kind, talking about your aunt like that.'

Abby grinned cheerfully, a wide puckered grin that lit the small sharp face with mischief.

'She doesn't like being called my aunt. I have to call her Luci. I only say Aunt Luci when I'm sure

she can't hear me.' Vienna decided it was probably
tactful not to comment, and Abby continued glee-
fully, 'Aunt Luci is my mother's very youngest
sister. Daddy was Uncle Bren's brother. I'm an
orphan, you know.'

'I'm sorry to hear that.'

The girl shrugged thin shoulders. 'Oh, it's not so
bad. I don't remember anything else, really. I was
only eighteen months old when my mother and
father died in an accident. Uncle Bren's my real
guardian, but Aunt Luci helps look after me, because I'm a girl.'

Vienna suggested tactfully, 'Perhaps you could
tell me something about what goes on in a cattle
station. Like, what time is breakfast, and what does
everybody like to eat?'

'You don't have to do it. Dorothy looks after
us.'

'I'll feel better if I help a bit,' Vienna answered
firmly. 'After all, we weren't really invited. At
least,' she added hurriedly, 'your uncle invited us,
but I feel a bit guilty. He really had us thrust on
him. So if you'll tell me what to do, maybe I could
help a little now and then.'

Abby spent the rest of the time in the kitchen
chattering happily about life in the outback. She
had a quick intelligence, and Vienna found herself
laughing at some of her comments. Once Abby
asked, 'Is it all right if I call you Vee, like your
boy-friend?' and Vienna said,

'Why not? Everybody else does.'

But of course it wasn't true. Not everybody
called her Vee or Vienna at all. The boss-man of
Glenister Two was being very careful about that.
Vienna wondered why she especially noticed his
omission. It didn't matter all that much. He could

call her anything he liked, just so long as he hurried up with repairing the car so they could go home quickly.

As they left the kitchen Abby said gravely, 'I like talking to you.'

'Thank you. I've enjoyed our talk, too.'

Soft music filled the big sitting room as Abby and Vienna entered, but the room was empty. There was neither sound nor movement on the darkened verandah outside.

'Gone for a walk,' Abby commented wisely. 'I know Aunt Luci. Bet she's taken him to look at the swimming pool or get all romantic around the frangipanni trees. They're smelly old trees, but some people like them.'

'You might grow fond of them yourself when you're a few years older,' Vienna laughed. 'That smell might turn into delicious perfume.'

'I shouldn't think so.' As Vienna settled herself in a comfortable chair, Abby moved restlessly between the record-player and a divan under curtained windows. 'I don't like things other people like. I have a—a personality problem.'

Vienna brought her attention sharply from the music.

'Whoever told you that, Abby?'

'Aunt Luci.' The softly-lit room showed Abby's rather shamefaced attempt at a smile. 'It was because I ran away,' she confessed.

'Not a very bright idea. Whatever made you do that?'

'I got fed up.' The taut little face twisted wryly. 'Like I told you, I'm an orphan.'

'Yes, you told me.'

'It's not all that dreadful, except that I have to live with Aunt Luci, so I can go to school in Adelaide.'

'Don't you like school?'

'I like school all right. That's the trouble. I'd rather be a boarder, not just a day-student; and I want to spend the holidays with my girl friends, but Luci won't let me. She drags me up here every chance she gets, so she can see lots of Uncle Bren, and I hate it. Why can't I go with my own friends? So I ran away.' She sighed unhappily. 'Of course, Aunt Luci came running after me, and brought me back. And here I am.' She managed a watery smile.

Vienna said carefully, 'Have you talked to your uncle about doing what you want?'

Abby twisted her hands together miserably.

'I'm not very good at talking to Uncle Bren,' she confessed. 'He's sort of bossy—you know, kind of overwhelming. He really spooks me.'

'Spooks!' The expression made Vienna give an involuntary laugh. If ever a man looked substantial, it was Bren Darcour.

'Sure. That's what they say about cattle, when they get the jitters and start stamping around. They're spooked.'

'Oh. Well, I'm sure your uncle doesn't mean to spook you.'

'He is bossy, though, isn't he?'

Vienna hesitated. 'A little dictatorial, perhaps,' she agreed carefully. 'I suppose he's used to giving orders. Why don't you tell yourself that your uncle has a—a personality problem, too? Maybe he doesn't listen enough to other people. So you'll have to be extra patient, and make him listen to you. Tell him it's important, and explain how you feel, that you'd rather be spending holidays with your school friends, instead of coming here. It's worth a try, isn't it?'

When Abby continued to look doubtful, Vienna tried to convince her.

'Bossy people have one-way communication. Make him listen. Keep cool, and don't let him fuss you.'

Abby gave another exaggerated sigh.

'He's going to be pretty cross, though,' she mourned. 'I mean, Luci took me away from school straight off, and rushed me up here to explain myself—about running away, I mean. I think she wants Uncle Bren to lecture me.' Her voice quavered. 'I don't like being lectured.'

'I think you may find your uncle a lot more understanding than you expect, Abby. I'd try talking to him if I were you.'

Abby produced another woeful expression.

'All right, I'll have a go,' she consented, 'If you really think it'll work. But I don't find him all that agreeable. Or Aunt Luci either.' She sniffed. 'I'll try, Vienna, I truly will. I'll ask him tomorrow.'

Outside, in the darkness of the verandah, Vienna thought she saw a shadowy movement, a fleeting change in the quality of velvet blackness.

Myra had let it be known that the day had been an ordeal for her and she intended going to her room for an early sleep immediately after dinner. Neil and Luci were supposedly walking in the garden. How very embarrassing, if the master of Glenister Two had overhead her comments on his dictatorial attitude.

Vienna allowed herself a wry smile, shakily bolstering her morale. Serves him right for eavesdropping, she tried to console herself, but it wasn't really any consolation.

She let Abby put another record on the player, but rejected the suggestion they might dance. Her feet, like her spirits, dragged heavily.

She stayed with Abby a little longer, then suggested bedtime. Neither Neil nor Luci reappeared. Whatever they were doing out there in the perfumed garden that should have been Red Vistas', they were certainly not in any hurry to return.

The bedrooms were located all along one side of the long passage, each with a door from the passage and another leading to the verandah outside. From inside the darkness of her room, Vienna glanced out through her half-opened door. A light still shone in the small room at one end of the verandah that Abby had pointed out as Brenden Darcour's office. At the other end, a faint red light glowed, like the moving end of a lighted cigarette, as if the man with the distant eyes might possibly be standing there, looking out over the night-shapes in the garden, at the black silk sky with its generous sprinkling of glittering stars.

Of Neil and Luci there was still no sign. Vienna silently closed the door and went back into her room, and when she switched on the light a beam of gold spilled out on to the dark verandah through her window. The distance man would know she was going to bed. She supposed he knew almost everything that went on in his vast domain, and wondered uneasily what he thought about Neil and Luci walking together in the shadows of the scented garden, and whether he minded.

Not really, she supposed. He seemed so very sure of himself. But she wouldn't care to be Neil if the granite jawed man should decide to consider him an enemy. Nor herself, either, if he should decide to direct his hostility her way.

She recalled the spurning cold of those dismissive grey eyes, and when she got into bed she pulled the sheet up close around her chin, as if for protection. It wasn't much in the way of armour, a cool flowered sheet that covered her slim body, clinging to the rounded curves of firm breasts, accepting the fall of thick black hair that cascaded down over the pillow's edge.

She didn't feel much like the cool, competent nurse who had offered skill and compassion and comfort to Evelyn Harryn in the last months of her life. She was feeling unusually vulnerable. Even when she turned over on her side to sleep, she kept the loose sheet covering her.

A few minutes later, the man on the verandah stubbed out his cigarette and walked slowly back to his office. He trod carefully, his light footsteps making little sound on the wooden boards, as if he might have taken special care not to disturb the sleep of tired travellers.

Outside in the garden a bird called, the penetrating mournful call of a hunting owl. The man threw back his head and stood quite still, listening. Then he walked on towards his office, and as he opened the door and stood in the rectangle of golden light, his hawklike profile showed sharp and clear.

For a little time, not more than the ticking of half a minute, he paused in the doorway, looking out into the shadowy garden, his face inscrutable. Then he went inside and closed the door.

CHAPTER FOUR

NEXT morning Vienna stood at her window watching the piccaninny dawn before she joined Dorothy in the kitchen to help with breakfast.

Above each bedroom doorway, a panel of skylight had been let into the sloping roof, so that the verandah at this time was striping with varying shades of shadow, light and dark; and Vienna found herself wondering behind which door the master of Glenister Two slept, or whether he slept on this side of the homestead at all.

She dressed in a swinging coloured skirt and slim black top, then tied her hair in a swathe of black ponytail that peeled off the years, so that she looked almost a child. But she was able to cope with breakfast, and even found time to carry Myra's meal in to her room on a tray.

Neil's mother responded wonderfully to pampering. She assured Vienna that she expected a pleasant holiday at Glenister, thanks to that wonderful Mr Darcour, so perhaps the expedition wouldn't be a total loss after all, and wasn't that a good thing? Her arch expression conveyed that Vienna had been sadly at fault, leading them all on this wild goose chase; but since she, Myra, now looked like being treated in the luxury to which she was accustomed at home, she intended holding no grudges.

However, she also managed to convey by steely-sweetness, Vienna had better watch her step in future ... her track record wasn't exactly perfection.

To her astonishment Vienna found she didn't really care. She asked, 'You'll let me know if there's anything else you want, won't you?' and Neil's mother said yes, she certainly would.

After breakfast, Vienna cleaned up in the kitchen. Brenden Darcour found her there. From the corners of her eyes Vienna saw him come in. He lounged easily just inside the doorway.

'Dorothy tells me you've rostered yourself for duty.'

She busied herself hanging cups on hooks, refusing to look at him.

'It's no trouble. I may as well do something while we're here.'

His footsteps came closer. She found herself conscious of his nearness, as if her heartbeats listened for his; and she shook away the thought indignantly, stubbornly refusing to turn and look at him.

'You don't have to work yourself to death just to prove whatever point you're making, Sister Maddern. I'm quite sure you're an extremely useful young woman. With your training you'd have to be, wouldn't you?'

Fiercely she turned on him, a cup in each hand, her mouth angry as her feelings; and something in the bland grey eyes told her this was just what he had intended. He'd goaded her into giving him her undivided attention.

With an angry curl of her lips, she flounced away and hung up the cups, all the time uncomfortably aware that he stood there, watching.

'Miss Maddern,' he said at last with exaggerated patience, 'I'm sure Dorothy is glad of your help. In fact, I know she is—very grateful. In return, we at

Glenister Two would like you to take a little time off to savour our—er—delightful charms, if you're inclined to this sort of thing. After all, you may not see it again.'

'I'm sure I shan't.' Vienna kept her voice crisp. 'I can promise you I don't intend to. And I'm sorry we've inflicted ourselves on you.'

He raised those fine eyebrows in mock exasperation. 'You're a prickly guest, aren't you? I really came to explain that I'll be away all day. I'm taking Luci out to one of the mustering camps. You're invited——'

Vienna shook her head.

'No, thank you.'

'In that case, perhaps you won't mind if young Abby stays with you. She seems to prefer your company.'

His features remained carefully impassive. If he referred to the conversation she and Abby had held the previous evening—if he really *had* been listening—he didn't intend telling her so.

Vienna answered as calmly as she could, 'I'll be pleased to look after Abby. What time do you want your evening meal?'

'We'll be back just after sundown, but don't panic—we'll have a barbecue. Oh, and I nearly forgot—your fiancé is coming with us. I hope you won't find things too desolate without him.'

Glumly, Vienna watched him walk away. Naturally he'd had the better of the interview, just as he probably got the better of most things.

She fitted the last of the plates into the rack, hastily swept the floor, and stamped outside. Abby lay on a recliner on the verandah reading, not very happily. She said contritely, 'I'll help you clear up next time, Vee. But I was so cross this morning. I actually got around to asking Uncle Bren if I could talk to him, and he brushed me off. Said he was too busy just now because he's driving out to the muster camp with Luci and that feller—your boy-friend.' She glanced apologetically at Vienna. 'I guess you hate me,' she finished, her lips drooping. 'I didn't mean to be rude about your—your boy-friend. But there's something about this place that makes me uptight. I guess it's the heat and dust—all that red sand and stuff—I just don't like it.'

Vienna stepped to the verandah's edge and peered out at the greens and vibrant colours of the garden.

'I can't imagine why you dislike it, Abby. It looks beautiful. Although I do see what you mean by what's outside the garden. It's dusty but fas-cinating. Anyhow, couldn't we find something interesting to do?'

Abby threw down her book. 'What is there that's interesting in a place like this?' Her mouth drooped moodily.

'How about a swim if you're hot?'

'All right, but not in the pool. Vee, could we walk down to the big waterhole? It's not all that far.'

Animation did attractive things to Abby's sharp features. The tiny plain face lost its look of secret discontent and came alive with pleasure.

Vienna said cheerfully, 'Okay, we'll walk. But first I'd better explain to Myra where we're going.'

Abby's waterhole was the largest of a chain, mostly shallow now because of the long dry season; a collection of straggling holes being all that remained of a river.

'In the Wet,' Abby remembered, 'it simply tears along in torrents. All frothing and—and horrible!'

'It's not horrid now, Abby. Let's have our swim, shall we?'

On the dry sand of the riverbed there were several clear footprints, and Vee pointed them out to Abby. 'Someone has been here before us.'

'Probably some of the Aborigines. There's a camp not all that far away. Most people use the riverbed for travelling during the dry season, it's much easier than walking around rocks and mulga and stuff.'

The waterhole was wide and mirror-calm, with two river red gums, side by side, looking down placidly at their own spreading reflections. A flock of grey and white birds made a small fluttering as they approached the far side of the pool.

'Quarrions,' Abby announced. 'Cockatoo-parrots . . . Uncle Bren calls them cockatiels.'

The quarrions settled down to look for food in the sparse grass a short distance from the waterhole.

Vienna said, 'It's beautiful, Abby. I truly can't think why you don't like it.'

'This bit's all right.' Abby dived neatly under the water and came up close to a gigantic rock. 'But look around you. Isn't it boring? Rocks and sand and trees—that's all it is.'

'You're spoiled, because you've seen it all your life, but I've never seen anything as exciting as this before. The light's so clear, the colour's so vivid. I can't understand how you could get bored, honestly, Abby.'

'It's Luci's fault.' Abby trod water, watching the movements of her arms under the surface. 'She won't let me do anything I want to do.'

After the swim, as they dried themselves in the shade of one of the trees, Abby came back to the subject of Luci.

'She gets a big fat allowance for having me live with her. If I went to school as a boarder, like my friends, she wouldn't get it—I know, because I heard her talking to one of her smart friends. And—and maybe she wouldn't have such a grand house, and all her smart friends wouldn't come to parties——' Seeing Vienna's disapproval Abby added desperately, 'All right, you think I'm un- grateful, just like the rest of them, and Uncle Bren too. But how would you like it if you had to be a day-girl instead of a boarder, and then some day I'm supposed to go to university and study, and I'll hate it. I know I will. I want to be an artist, and paint and sketch things—a book illustrator, maybe—not like some dumb old professor reading books.'

'Why don't you try sketching around here? This would be a great place to keep your hand in. I was looking at that magnificent tree, thinking how I'd like to draw it. Only I didn't bring a sketchbook with me.'

'It's a river red gum.' Abby hesitated. 'Are you an artist?'

Vienna laughed. 'No, afraid not. But I did have to decide between graphic arts and nursing after I left secondary school, and I decided I'd make a better nurse—fortunately, because I'm no genius. But I get a lot of fun from sketching. What a pity I didn't bring any materials with me, we might have gone on a couple of excursions together.'

'You don't need to have things with you.' Abby's eyes were alive and shining. 'Do you truly mean it, Vee? Because if you do we'll find something in the store. There's sure to be paper and pads, pencils, and lots of other things we can use.'

Her thin hands were clasped together with excitement. Vienna shook her head warningly.

'You won't be impressed with my efforts, Abby. I haven't done much for a long time. But I can see a few things here I wouldn't mind trying to sketch—rocks, mulga trees, all those weird shapes they tangle themselves into.'

Abby could hardly wait to get back and ransack the store for materials. Vienna saw with misgiving that she had collected a huge bundle of notepads that would do very well as sketchbooks, and what seemed a vast quantity of pens and pencils.

Vienna gave Myra a salad lunch, and as Neil's mother seemed content to sit on the verandah and read, she and Abby went again to the waterhole, this time to sketch.

Towards the end of the afternoon a few Port Lincoln parrots, emerald green and yellow, fluttered down to drink and an owl—a tawny frogmouth—forgot his nocturnal habits and sat on a branch, squinting at them out of slit eyes.

Abby was a perfectionist. She designed carefully, with meticulous attention to detail, yet all her drawings had a strongly individual touch. She had talent, Vienna decided, turning the pages of her sketchbook respectfully.

'I think you have a gift, Abby,' she said. 'If you want to do something creative with it, then I believe you really ought to battle to go the way you want to.'

Vienna herself had facility. She sketched swiftly, sometimes to catch something she considered graceful or curious, sometimes with an impish sense of humour making caricature sketches.

'I like your pictures,' Abby giggled. 'I'm glad you're here.'

All the way back to the homestead Abby chattered. Reticence gone, she became entertaining and amusing, and Vienna found herself responding with a mixture of affection and compassion. It was the same feeling she had had for Evelyn Harryn.

Once or twice, as Abby detailed some episode she found amusing in the apparently relentless pursuit of Glenister Two's master by her Aunt Luci, Vienna had to tactfully steer the conversation to something else. Brenden Darcour, she felt certain, would not even be slightly amused to hear his amorous adventures described by the irreverent and sometimes, she suspected, highly imaginative tongue of his niece.

That Luci fancied herself in the position of mistress of Glenister was obvious from her tactics that evening after the barbecue. When they all went in to the sitting room for coffee she left Neil to entertain Vienna and his mother whenever Bren Darcour entered the room.

And that Bren Darcour fancied Luci was also obvious. He had calls coming through on the transceiver throughout the evening, but whenever he returned he danced with Luci to the records Abby played, and his hard face lost its expression of remoteness and severity as he glanced down at her and answered her teasing with pleasure and obvious interest.

Luci had sexual attraction and she had personality. She was greedy, too; she didn't intend sharing the man she wanted with anybody. She hung on to his arm and raised her bright face to his whenever a record finished, talking vivaciously, so that it was practically impossible for another person to break into the closed conversation.

Bren was sexy, too. Vienna hadn't realised it

before. Powerful, yes; but until tonight the granite-faced man with the chilly eyes had radiated not one vibration that spelled sex appeal or warmth or the potential for passion ... Until he danced with Luci, and Luci beamed the full power of her sophisticated art on to him, and the hard mouth curved into laughter, grey eyes defrosted, crinkling into warmth where there had been only wintry cold. And not for anyone but Luci ...

This man would make a forceful lover ... Whatever am I thinking of? Vienna drew back from the impulsive thought with alarm. She was glad he hadn't asked her to dance. Nobody wanted to be turned on by somebody who couldn't care less ... Deliberately, she turned to talk to Myra, and when she looked up again the music had stopped and Abby was making her special request.

'Uncle Bren, next time you go to your office, may I come with you? I have something special to ask you. I mean, I think I should talk——'

She said it clearly, without faltering except at the end when resolution faltered. When she'd finished, her eyes searched frantically across the room for Vienna's encouragement.

The big man hesitated. A little of the severity had come back into his expression.

'Is it important?'

Abby wavered. Luci shot her a venomous look that might have quelled; then Abby swallowed painfully, and straightened thin, childish shoulders.

'Yes, it is. It's very important.'

'In that case we'd better talk. Whenever you like, Abby. Why not now?'

Luci smiled with spurious brightness.

'I'd better come,' she carolled. 'After all, I'm

partly responsible for Abby, aren't I?'

Abby's face crumpled, but Bren carefully disengaged Luci's clinging fingers from his shirt-sleeve.

'I take it this one is strictly for me?' He raised his eyebrows, and Abby nodded. He had been so careful not to look at Vienna, but she knew he had been subtly aware of every exchanged glance, of Abby's eyes beseeching, as she hunted desperately for her support across the room.

He had been careful to erase every revealing expression from his own features, but of course he had overhead their conversation last night; Vienna was sure of it now.

He ordered calmly, 'Come on, Abby,' and to Myra, 'You'll excuse us?' and Luci flounced to the divan where Neil sat, and perched beside him, swinging one foot against a nearby chair-leg. She kicked at it spitefully until she saw Vienna watching her, then she satisfied herself with a swift turnabout into charm, doing her best to captivate Neil and his mother.

Vienna was finding Neil extraordinarily quiet. He hadn't offered to dance with her, nor had he exchanged more than a few casual remarks. She still wore his ring on her finger, and if Neil was disenchanted with the engagement he had rushed into he gave no other sign than this faint, polite withdrawal.

Perhap he was weary. Perhaps he lavished most of his attention on his mother because he felt guilty that the expedition had turned into such a debacle. Perhaps.

Vienna twisted the ring aimlessly on her fingers, and flushed as she saw both Neil and Luci watching. She gave them a determined bright smile to divide between them as they pleased, before she strolled across to the record cabinet to find something to play while Abby battled through her interview with Bren.

But it was a surprisingly short interview. Vienna chose a classical record, a selection of Chopin piano pieces, because the lilting, haunting music never failed to captivate her imagination. The notes still cascaded into the room like spring sunshine when Abby and Bren came back.

Luci darted across the room and petulantly demanded, 'Something we can dance to, and a drink, for heaven's sake!' while Abby took her seat again on the arm of Vienna's chair, much of the strain erased from her sharp little face.

'He says I can't be a boarder,' she managed to whisper to Vienna. 'I have to go on living with Luci a few more years. But I can choose where I spend my hols. And Vee——' a deep shining flashed in her eyes, a gleaming strangely reminiscent of the brightness in Bren's eyes as he laughed down at Luci—as she confided in a whisper, 'I can be an artist, a book illustrator or anything I want to be, if I'm good enough to get accepted at art school!'

Vienna watched the glow in Abby's face, the excited quivering mouth. 'Two out of three isn't bad,' she encouraged.

'Two out of three is fantastic. Fabulous!' Abby's face shone. 'Can we do some more sketches tomorrow, Vee? I told him—Uncle Bren—that we were practising, and he said he was pleased to hear it. And we don't have to pay for any of the pads and stuff from the store. He'll put it down to office expenses.'

Vienna said quietly, 'That's great, Abby.' But she

didn't think it was great. She didn't want to be beholden to the man with the scathing attitude any more than she had to, and now it seemed that everything she did put her further in his debt.

He was ignoring her now, bending his head to listen while Luci talked, giving her his undivided attention so that nobody else in the room seemed to matter to him. Vienna didn't know why the sight piqued her. She fought away her growing awareness of the man she detested, and transferred her attention to the collection of Aboriginal artefacts around the room. A collection of long spears with carved wooden blades hung above the bar, and there were several cabinets containing beautifully decorated pieces of carved woodwork. Each piece was covered with complex designs, some burnt on to the smoothed, carved wood, others obviously chiselled or engraved.

She left her chair and stood admiring. Abby said indifferently, 'They're Aboriginal things, from the camp I told you about.'

Carefully, Vienna picked up a small carved lizard, tracing the scaly patterns on its back with her fingers.

Abby told her, 'You can get some of those if you want to. Some of them are made to send away and sell to tourists; but Uncle Bren always chooses the ones he wants to buy.'

'It's beautifully carved, isn't it? It must have taken hours. And don't you love the designs?'

Abby shrugged. She'd seen them all before. But Vienna stood admiring, touching the dramatised patterns of snakes and lizard-scales, of wildflowers and vines and animals and mystic symbols . . .

'It must take hours to make them.' She replaced

the lizard back on the shelf. 'Are they made from bark?'

'No. They're all carved out of tree trunks and branches. That's why they're so strong, they're hollowed out of blocks of wood.'

The record stopped, and Vienna heard Luci's quick footsteps across the polished floor towards the player. Neil said something and Myra replied. Vienna faced the cabinet with its crowded shelves, isolated from all of them, even Abby, because she knew that Bren Darcour stood behind her; and it appalled her that she was so certain of his nearness although she could not see him.

He took his time before speaking. Then at last the ironic voice drawled, 'Looking for a weapon, Miss Maddern?'

Keep cool, she ordered herself. Don't let him throw you . . . That was what she'd advised Abby. Keep cool and don't let him fuss you. Now she repeated it to herself with vigour.

She forced her voice to say coolly, 'Not especially a weapon, although I must admit they're tempting. Abby tells me everything is carved from trees.'

'That's right.'

'It's exquisite work, isn't it?'

She half turned, so that he could see her cool green eyes and her soft curving mouth that she had forbidden to show any sign of her inner turmoil.

He took a long time about answering, as though it pleased him to keep her standing there while his grey eyes scanned her features as if he searched for something.

'Yes, wonderful artistry.'

He said it briefly, as if he were not going to talk about it, only Luci and Neil and Myra came across the room and joined them and Luci commented,

'You've added more to your collection.'

'Yes—a few more digging baskets, and some spear-throwers and body-shields. A few other things as well. I'll have to get more shelves next time I'm down south. I might order a display case.'

The digging baskets, called coolamons, were curved oval receptacles, hollowed out of branches, the undersides covered with strange patterns of whirls and curves, or rhythmic designs of flowers and grasses. On one, an emu's head stared haughtily at a coiled snake; on others there were wildlfowers linked by trailing vines into suggestive and tantalising mysteries.

Neil picked up two cigar-shaped objects of solid wood, each about ten inches long, covered with swirling, mysterious markings.

'Aboriginal mini-torpedoes,' he suggested flippantly.

Bren's eyes became icy. 'Music makers,' he answered shortly. 'They're clapped together, to make rhythms.' He shot Neil a look of distaste.

Vienna asked hastily, 'Are they made from special trees?'

'Whatever's available. The snake on the wall is carved from mulga. Eucalypts, desert oak—they're all utilised. Some of the longest spears are made out of tree roots, long, strong roots, straightened and treated, of course.'

'And they're strong enough to kill an animal?'

'They'd kill a man,' he answered with a grim smile.

Vienna queried, 'The designs on the baskets and lizards are burnt on?'

'That's right.' Bren replaced the artefacts on the shelves. 'I don't know how it was done in the old days, but I saw old Gracie using a heated piece of wire coathanger the other day, burning snake designs on to her basket.'

'Doesn't she have an Aboriginal name?'

'If she did, the chances are you wouldn't be able to pronounce it. Most Aboriginal languages have very complex sounds, very tongue-tangling.'

'Do the women make all the articles?'

'No. Women make what women use. Men carve the objects used by men.'

'Sounds reasonable.' Vienna turned a digging basket gently in her hands. 'Sorry to ask so many questions, but I'm fascinated. Are they sacred objects?'

Half smiling, he shook his head.

'If they were, they wouldn't be here. They'd be hidden in secret places, guarded by spirits.' He touched one of the spears thoughtfully. 'The Aboriginal people know how to keep their secrets, and their dignity. These are everyday articles, the ones we are permitted to see and touch.'

Vienna picked up a delicately-made hollow vessel, decorated with flower patterns.

'What's this?'

'It's a breast-milk cup.'

He wasn't embarrassed. Neither was she. It was a special vessel, gracefully designed with curved lips to receive the milk from a woman's breast, its exterior adorned in flower shapes of fragile beauty.

Bren said unexpectedly, 'You can come to the camp with me one day, if you want to, and buy a few artefacts for yourself.'

'Yes, I will. Thank you.'

But Neil said, 'It's spooky-looking stuff, isn't it? I mean, all those snakes writhing around—I suppose they must signify something.'

Bren turned away swiftly, as if they might have

been aliens, all of them, denigrating his precious possessions; and so great was his dominance that they followed him meekly and sat down, all except Luci who darted over to the player to provide more dance music.

She beckoned, 'Dance, Bren. That's better than standing around,' and he went willingly to take her in his arms and smile down at her as he had smiled before.

She could have him! Vienna decided furiously. For a little while there, as he handled the artefacts with strong but gentle hands, she had sensed a bond of sympathy, as though there might have been between them a shared reverence for the hours of hard work, the painstaking discipline that turned tree-trunks into hollow baskets and fashioned spears out of tree roots, covering them all with haunting patterns that stirred the imagination.

Then Luci had beckoned and the fragile bond was broken. So quickly. So definitely. As if it had never been there.

Vienna stared resentfully at the carved wooden snake. So she had imagined it all ... so she had ...

She called crisply, 'Anyone for supper? Tea or coffee?'

And Brenden Darcour, not even pausing from the rhythm of his dancing, turned to Abby and said, 'You can make tea or coffee, can't you, Abigail? We can't have Miss Maddern working all the time.'

Miss Maddern ... not Vienna. Nor Vee ... Come to think of it, he was still insultingly careful not to use her first name. Anything else. Miss Maddern ... Sister Maddern ... even the in-flammatory 'Nursie' ... So careful to keep distance between them, he made the easy use of his own name impossible for her.

Neil talked in a low voice with his mother. Luci's arm curled around Bren's elbow and settled there, with curved clutching fingers, like a caterpillar clinging to a leaf.

Vienna announced tersely, 'No supper for me, thank you, Abby. I'm tired. I think I'll go to bed.'

She moved abruptly towards the door, after a falsely bright goodnight, and nobody made the slightest attempt to stop her.

CHAPTER FIVE

NEXT morning there was no mention of a visit to the Aboriginal camp. Bren and Luci went out to the muster again, but this time they rode.

Luci wore a dashing outfit in gold and black, but it was the big man who caught the eye, as usual. The casual gear he wore—slim-legged trousers, riding boots, a green and black shirt and broad-brimmed hat—accentuated the power of the body underneath as he rode the chestnut stallion that was apparently his special mount. He sat with lithe grace, well in command, man and horse moving together with the understanding of two who have formed a strong bond after long and satisfactory association.

The horse pricked his ears at the light, bright morning, as if anxious to be away, and his rider also had the preoccupied air of someone who is already elsewhere in his thinking.

Perversely, Vienna dressed in the navy shirt and white cotton skirt she had worn on the first day of their travelling. She knew it looked drab beside Luci's arresting outfit and the knowledge did nothing to lift her spirits.

She asked, 'Where to today, Abby?' and Abby said, 'It's going to be awfully hot. Could we just stay around the house and the swimming pool?'

So they swam in the chlorinated pool, its sterile blue water in strange contrast to the duskier colours of yesterday's waterhole.

Neil had not been invited to ride. He was inclined

to sulk at first, but after a splash in the pool with Vienna and Abby he thawed sufficiently to cast appreciative glances at Vee, who had changed the skirt and blouse for a turquoise one-piece swimsuit with shell-pink drawstrings.

Even Abby looked impressed. She surveyed Vienna from toes to the top of her head, then she said primly, 'You have a really great figure, Vee.'

Vienna had to laugh. 'Thanks. It's kind of you to notice.'

She and Abby giggled together, but Abby's laughter was fleeting. She said mournfully. 'When I grow up, I shan't bother about my figure.'

'Why ever not?'

Abby grinned shamefacedly. 'Well, I'm not the kind of chick to turn the fellers on, am I?'

'Whatever does that mean?'

'Sorry.' She sighed. 'What I really mean is—well, I'm not ever going to be a—a sex symbol, am I? Even in primary school the kids laughed at me. Stick-legs, they called me. Not that I cared.'

But she *had* cared. Shadows of remembered humiliations took the brightness from her face. She added stiffly. 'So I'd be pretty silly to bother much about my looks.'

'That's a pity. Most redheads grow up to be pretty dynamic, don't they? And your legs aren't sticks now. I was thinking how lucky you are to have those grey eyes with your colour hair. And your face is such an unusual shape. Still, if you don't think it's worth bothering——'

Trying not to see the pinched look around Abby's tight mouth, Vienna shrugged her shoulders, carefully casual. She picked up her sketchbook and Abby followed her example, and they both sat sketching for a few minutes.

When Abby looked up her face was pink. 'I suppose it's a bit early for making final decisions,' she announced. 'I mean, like you say, there's no reason why I shouldn't be an interesting-looking book illustrator, is there?'

'None whatsoever,' Vienna agreed calmly, sketching quickly before the sun played tricks with the shapes and shadows she was trying to capture.

Later, Vienna took Neil exploring the shade houses behind the homestead where Jo-Jo the gardener-yardman, had coaxed a quite remarkable number of vegetables and flowers into flourishing.

Joe Johnstone, called Jo-Jo, was Dorothy Green's father. Once head stockman, now permanently out of the saddle after a serious tractor accident, Jo-Jo spent most of his time creating the gardens around the homestead. 'Earthbound,' he called it with a chuckle, and if he sometimes looked wistfully after the sand-plumes of flying horsemen, he didn't let frustration interfere with his work.

Dorothy said that Bren regularly urged him to retire to the bungalow permanently his own on Glenister run; but with Jo-Jo, Dorothy added, to stop working would be to die. He busied himself with the soil, a spritely gnome of a man with laughing eyes and a quick tongue. He had a mop of grizzled curly hair, and silver-black tufted eyebrows that worked furiously all the time he talked. He stared at the piece of sage Vienna brought him.

'That's a handsome piece of nature's handiwork,' he scoffed. 'You won't start a plantation with that. I can offer you a better root.'

But Vienna refused his offer, and he produced a container and potting soil, and without further comment found a place for the sage bush on a shelf in one of his shade houses. Then he gave Neil and Vienna an escorted tour of the kitchen garden, the citrus grove and other shade houses, talking energetically all the time. Neil tagged along a few paces behind, without making any attempt to become involved. He didn't care for kitchen gardens, even for orchids or orange trees.

As they walked back he grumbled, 'What's so fascinating about a few things growing? The man has all day to look after them, hasn't he? So he ought to be good at it. I don't know why you have to spend time buttering him up.'

There were enough sore feelings about just now, so Vienna did her best to coax him into a happier mood. Then Abby appeared, looking lost and resentful, and Vienna sighed.

The heat wasn't improving anybody's outlook. Even Myra, fanning herself gently in her lounger on the verandah, had begun to wilt. She was storing up the experience to impress her friends in Adelaide, but Bren and Luci's continued absence she regarded as rather an affront. Myra expected to be treated as an honoured guest, and to be left reading on the verandah wasn't her idea of preferential treatment. While Bren did all he could to make her comfortable he wasn't nearly as deferential as she might have liked. Her eyes dwelt approvingly on her own son.

Vienna made salads for lunch, followed by sliced pineapple out of tins, topped with cream and passionfruit. Myra pronounced the dessert too rich, but she came back for seconds, and Abby frankly enjoyed every spoonful.

'Now,' she whispered like a conspirator, 'can we go and away and draw some more?'

Tactfully Vienna suggested they might try some

portraits, and they sat on the verandah later making sketches of Myra and Neil. Unexpectedly, Abby's talent blossomed in her drawings of people. She was unusually perceptive for her age, and her sketches had extra dimension. They were real people.

Perhaps Abby had been short-changed on appreciation in the past, because when Myra accepted her sketch with gracious approval, she turned scarlet and wriggled with embarrassment.

Vienna said, 'One of the nurses at the hospital designs all her own Christmas cards. Her friends keep them for ever,' and Abby flipped over the pages of her book, looking at what she had done, then she said, shrugging to keep it casual.

'You know, I just might try that.'

She was sketching Neil, and she began to work quickly and with confidence, and when it was finished the sketch deserved all the praise he gave it.

Although it was only November, and she would have plenty of time for designing Christmas cards, Abby couldn't wait after that. She went into Bren's office to see if there were any books on the shelves that might help with printing and lettering.

When it was almost time to think about the evening meal, Dorothy Green appeared.

'Don't worry about it,' Vienna told her cheerfully. 'Better let me do what I can while I'm here. Neil's car will be fixed and we'll be gone in a couple of days.'

'Are you sure?' Dorothy looked hesitantly at the sketchbook in Vienna's hand. 'You've got other things to do. Let's go into the kitchen, anyway, and see what we can find.'

They found steaks, and a good supply of Jo-Jo's

vegetables. Dorothy said, 'Look, if you don't mind, and this isn't too much imposition, I can arrange for a couple of the Aboriginal girls to help you. They're used to working in the house when we have visitors. If I didn't have the children's exams coming on, I wouldn't let you do it, but I'm truly grateful at this time.' She grinned. 'You really are a treasure.'

Vienna wrinkled her nose. 'Doesn't sound like me. And it's honestly no trouble. So if you don't object to me shrieking for help when I get lost, I'll be happy to take over the cooking while we're here, unless anybody complains. It's an easy kitchen to work in. Did you arrange the layout?'

Dorothy shook her head.

'No. Until a few years ago it was mostly as Bren's parents left it. Then Luci talked him into getting someone up from Adelaide to renovate. She wanted the sitting room and dining room reorganised, and the main bedroom; but Bren is a bit sentimental about those, so he settled for kitchen and laundry. He doesn't mind lesser changes in the rest of the homestead, like curtains and upholstery, but I think he's reluctant to change the way his parents furnished. He prefers things as they are.'

Dorothy shook her head ruefully. 'Luci's all for updating, and I wasn't very popular, I'm afraid, because I agreed with Bren that it oughtn't to be altered—not as drastically as Luci wanted, anyway. All that beautiful solid old furniture seems so right, here. I don't think Luci actually fancied herself working in the kitchen; it was the appearance she wanted to alter. But I don't believe Bren will ever change much at all, unless it wears out. Except for his artefacts, of course.'

'He's collected plenty of those, hasn't he?'

'He and his father both had tremendous appreciation for the work of Aboriginal craftsmen. Bren has a splendid relationship with most of them. Those are the only changes he makes willingly—when he adds to his collection he often has to buy more shelves and cabinets to house everything.'

Vienna said, surprised, 'He's conservative, then?'

Dorothy hesitated. 'Not so much conservative, but I think he's absorbed from the Aborigines a lot of their respect for time. In most of their beliefs, time is the basis for everything. Anything that has lasted ought to be respected. I don't know for sure that's the way Bren feels, but he seems to me to have that attitude.' She laughed selfconsciously. 'Here I am philosophising, putting reasons into the man's head I don't know were ever there! And whatever did we start with—a kitchen!'

At dinner that evening, Vienna looked around the large dining room with new interest. Of course, she had already noticed the porcelain chandelier with its delicate pink roses, and the gleam of carved wood on the high ceiling. But now she looked around her at the polished floor with its Indian rugs; the carved chairbacks, the enormous sideboard wearing the shine of years of polishing.

Anything that has lasted ought to be respected, Dorothy had said; and Vienna knew what she meant.

Bren looked down at her from the head of the table with ironically raised eyebrows, and to her annoyance, Vienna flushed and looked away.

He thinks I'm assessing, she decided furiously. Now he's decided I'm calculating how valuable everything is!

After that she focussed her attention deter-

minedly on the dinner table. She spoke when she
was spoken to. She half-listened to conversations,
because she was feeling ill at ease, and angry with
herself for reacting that way.

And when they moved into the sitting room for
coffee and liqueurs, she wished desperately that she
hadn't taken so much trouble to fill the bowls of
china and brass with flowers. Certainly the big man
noticed although he gave no sign. . . . Of course he
noticed: he was the boss-man, who noticed everything.

She had not taken one flower without Jo-Jo's
approval, but now the vases of fragrant frangipanni, the bowls of colourful bougainvillaeas,
suddenly lost their beauty for Vienna. They
shrieked at her. What right did she have to collect
armfuls of flowers from the garden so that she
could put her signature in rooms that were no concern of hers?

She had only intended to make them beautiful,
but it didn't look like that. She knew exactly how
it would look to the master of Glenister Two . . .

As if she were taking hold, insinuating herself
where she had no right to be. He had made it plain
he considered her avaricious. She was wearing the
cream and gold blouse she had worn the evening
he visited her flat, and he looked at her quickly, as
if he might have been remembering.

Restlessness was taking hold of Vienna. She
wanted to get away. Already they had been here
two days and there was no talk about the mechanic
travelling to Red Vistas to repair Neil's car. She
knew Terry was busy, and Dorothy too, but surely
something could be done.

As soon as she could, she collected coffee cups
and glasses, and she and Abby washed up; but

afterwards she couldn't settle back in the sitting room and listen to more records while Luci and Bren danced, and Neil withdrew into the sulkiness that came down over him now whenever Luci turned her attention to Bren.

Abby went to collect more materials from the store, and Vienna walked down the verandah steps into the garden. She wandered restlessly across to the pool, where the row of traveller's palms let through just enough moonlight to streak the water with broken bars of light. The recliners and deck-chairs had been folded up and put away, leaving an eerie feeling of emptiness and mystery, as though the night were unoccupied. Yet there was no knowing what might be lurking among the velvet shadows and pearly half-lights flung by the palms. From somewhere, a haunting bird-cry disturbed the night, and somewhere else a sudden rustling stirred the leaves of otherwise silent trees, as if some night creature scrambled among them.

Vienna looked around her doubtfully. She could go back inside, but she didn't really want to. She walked to the rock garden of daisy-flowers, now closing their bright faces in the dark, and then she sat carefully on a smooth granite boulder at one end of the rockery. She was still there half an hour later, dreaming, when Bren came down the verandah steps, feet crunching on the driveway as he walked around the swimming pool towards her.

He said, 'Do you find our company so tedious, Miss Maddern?' and she shook herself out of reverie and answered crisply, 'Of course not.'

He stood beside her, cupping his hands around a lighted match, and taking his time to draw on a cigarette before he asked lazily, 'I wonder what brings you out here, then?'

Vienna stood up quickly. She didn't like him standing there, looming over her.

He was a man of impact, sitting or standing, and she wished he would go away. The moon topped the palms and floated free, shining full on his face, but it didn't reveal anything of the thoughts that moved behind those shadowed eyes. Their expression was probably distant, as always. Luci seemed the only person for whom they thawed.

Certainly his voice was cool, almost unfriendly.

Vienna said stiffly, 'I'm sorry if you—and the others—got the wrong impression. I didn't come out here because I found the company boring. I simply felt—restless, I suppose. I needed to think.'

'I'm sure you did.' His voice was dry.

She lifted her head and stared at him in confusion.

'And what does that mean?'

'Your—ah—fiancé doesn't seem to be acting out his role to anywhere near perfection, does he? Not since he sighted the fair Luci, and what he probably hopes is her equally fair fortune. Or, should I say, not since he set eyes on what remains of your supposed inheritance at Red Vistas? Not quite as substantial a bequest as he expected, perhaps.'

Vienna turned on him furiously.

'You have no right to say things like that about a man, just because he can't hear you!'

Calmly he drew on his cigarette. Then he said musingly, 'I'm not saying them because he can't hear me. I'm saying them because they're true, and because you can hear. Tell me, what on earth possesses an otherwise intelligent young woman to set herself up with a shallow, conniving——'

The moonlight shone on his hair now, on the

silver sun-bleached streaks gleaming, even in the dark . . .

Set yourself up . . . those had been his words. They stung Vienna, so that she turned on him again, her feelings white-hot.

'What would you know about it?' she blazed. 'You don't understand anything about other people at all. You're—you're so darn self-satisfied, and arrogant—you know nothing whatever about other people and their feelings!'

There was a silence. Then Bren said, his voice hissing-soft, 'And you do?'

He was questioning her judgment, and because he touched sensitive nerve-ends, going straight to the vulnerable part of her emotions that had always doubted, she stared at him in baffled silence.

'What happened?' His voice was deadly quiet. 'What exactly did you do, Nursie? Panic when you turned twenty-one, and grab the first available male?'

She guessed he was goading her, but she couldn't imagine why. Perhaps it was bottled-up disappointment, anxiety—and yes, her shame, because she knew she ought not to be here. Her control exploded in one flash of anger that set her right hand reaching out, and before she actually made any decision she did something she had never done before; she slapped a person's face. Bren Darcour's face . . .

It wasn't easy, because he was so much taller than she was, but she managed it—a stinging blow that even in the dim light brought a flare of colour on to one side of his sunbrowned face.

It must have hurt him, because the impact stung her palm. Vienna stared at him aghast. Hypnotised, she watched the mask of anger settle over his face. With a quick movement he tossed the lighted

cigarette into the swimming pool, and she heard
the hiss of burning tobacco striking water.

He took one step towards her.

'If it's physical contact you want, Sister
Maddern——' he gritted, and reached for her.
Galvanised into action, Vienna twisted on one heel,
but the daisies caught her feet. She would have
careered into the granite boulder she had used for
a seat, but his long arms reached out and twisted
her away. Not to safety. He had rescued her from
the rock because he had other indignities to inflict
upon her.

He half pushed, half carried her down on to the
rock-garden, and almost in the same movement she
felt the whole of his weight on her slim body, pressing her back on to the uneven ground. She
became painfully, achingly aware of every pebble,
every tough fibre of knotted growth, even the cold
hard bud of a flower pressing on one cheek as she
twisted in panic to get away from him.

With one strong hand he held her jaw, im-
mobilising her. With the other he reached for the
front of her blouse. She heard the tearing of silk.
She felt his fingers, then, strong on her throat; one
arm hard and powerful holding her down while his
mouth searched the soft white curve of her shoulder, searching and finding her breast.

Jabbing into her back, a sharp-edged rock sent
waves of pain across her shoulderblades every time
she twisted in an effort to evade her tormenter.
She heard a voice—surely her own voice—draw
ragged sobbing breaths, crying out pain; then even
that sound was silenced as he lifted his head and
took possession of her mouth.

It was unbelievable, that she could be so easily
conquered. Incredible, too, that when his kissing

changed from punishment to persuasion, she should feel through her fear and anger a touch of sweetness, a faint promise of pleasure that hovered somewhere between sensuality and something deeper.

But the helplessness was frightening, and when he took his lips away from hers she fell back limply, without resistance. Over the shoulders that pushed her down, she saw the wide, stiff fan of a traveller's palm against the sky. The dark shape wavered and blurred until it became a swimming shadow in a world that reeled around her like something out of control.

Then, suddenly, it was all over. She felt Bren's grip slacken.

'Oh, lord!' he groaned, and his arms curved around her, picking her up and cradling her as if she had been a weeping child. He stroked her hair and smoothed the slender stem of her neck, bending his head so that her face was tucked protectively into the hollow of his shoulder. Clearly, she heard the steady thumping of his heart. He rocked her gently, sharing his strength with her, and as she relaxed Vienna found herself recalling vividly the nights she had spent with her arms curved like this around Evelyn Harryn or some other grieving patient, in the dark times when grief had been too strong for them to bear alone.

Sometimes in this way, in compassion, she had offered the warmth and strength of her young body to infuse comfort and confidence. This time, she was the receiver. She let the soothing warmth of Bren Darcour flow into her bruised body until her breathing quietened, and she became herself again, in control as she liked to be. Then she pushed experimentally against the encircling arms. He let her go; and while she wrapped the torn blouse around her he watched silently, only reaching out to help as she struggled to fit a wrenched button into a torn buttonhole with shaking fingers.

He didn't apologise. She knew he was appalled by the fury of his own anger, and the way it had broken the curb of his control. He lifted her, slowly and carefully, keeping his strengthening arm around her shoulders as they walked back through the moonlight to the homestead.

On the verandah outside her bedroom door, he asked quietly, 'Are you all right? I mean, do you need anything? Liniment for your bruises? Brandy for your spirits?' His smile was twisted.

Vienna shook her head.

'I don't need anything,' she assured him.

She wanted to tell him not to worry, that what happened was partly her fault, but her throat closed on the words.

And later, after a hot shower that she hoped would ease the bruising and scratches on her back, she lay on her bed recalling all the sensations, the cruelty and the tenderness; and she knew that whatever else she did when she got back to Adelaide, she must give Neil back his ring. The admiration she had felt for him, the pleasure in whatever attentions he granted her, were only pale sensations compared with the quality and intensity of emotion the big man with the grey eyes had been able to arouse in her.

Maybe some day she would experience that kind of feeling in a lasting relationship with some other man. Until she did, there was no way she could settle for less.

Not if I have to wait until the day I die, she promised herself fiercely, and was shaken to find herself wondering whether life without that feeling could become unbearable desolation.

Myra Rensome glanced at Vienna curiously next morning. Perhaps it was the purple shadows around her eyes, the strain-lines that refused to disappear entirely under make-up.

Some time, Vienna thought idly, she must borrow needle and thread from Dorothy Green and get to work on the torn blouse.

Bren had already left for the stock camp, though he was to come back to the homestead for the afternoon, Luci said.

The atmosphere around the breakfast table was strained. Luci and Neil planned to go riding, and there had been some discussion with Bren about the horse Neil was to saddle up. Neil looked sulky. His handsome face with its smooth dark hair wore the thunderous expression that came over it sometimes when things went wrong at the hospital. He was looking for someone to blame.

Vienna wondered whether Bren had been needling him, or whether he had perhaps deliberately selected a horse Neil didn't expect to feel comfortable riding. She wouldn't be surprised. There was a definite lack of empathy between the two men, and the boss of Glenister must be sick and tired of their enforced company. No doubt he would feel entitled not to become obliging if Neil made unreasonable requests.

Perhaps he suspected Neil of trying to impress Luci, and resented it. In any event, he must have been dictatorial with his orders, because Neil went off with Luci to the saddling paddock, looking moody and displeased.

Although Neil did casually invite Vienna to join

them for the ride, he was obviously indifferent about her refusal, even a little relieved; and Myra said sweetly that of course dear Vienna didn't want to go, she had her duties in the homestead, hadn't she? And the child Abigail needed her company while Luci was away.

After they had gone Vienna asked, 'Abby, did you want to ride?'

Abby shook her head.

'With them?' Her voice was scornful. 'No, thanks!'

Vienna supposed she ought to offer some sort of rebuke, but she was tired, and despite a second warm shower the bruises on her back ached and there was some slight stiffness. She would have preferred to stretch out in the garden in some green and shady place where the heat could not reach her. But Abby wanted to make more sketches.

She had already designed Christmas cards with drawings of the homestead, the gardens, some river red gums and all the odd rock shapes she could find.

'Let's take our swimsuits and have a dip at the waterhole before we start work,' she pleaded, and Vienna almost said yes, until she remembered the marks on her back.

There was no way she could screen them from Abby's curious eyes once she got into her swimsuit So she had no choice but to sit around on the bank with her sketchbook while Abby frolicked in the water. Her skin grew damp and prickly in the heat, and her temper became correspondingly scratchy. Every so often she had to move, chasing small patches of shade on the bank, so it wasn't long before she was really sticky and uncomfortable; and she thought wrathfully that if Luci wanted

Glenister Two she was welcome to it, and she could have the boss-man as well!

Next time she moved, chasing elusive shade, Vienna disturbed a frill-necked lizard sunning himself on a slab of rock. The creature reared up on its hind legs, grimacing hideously, expanding his neck-frill like an Elizabethan ruff around his throat. Grotesquely, he pranced backwards, mouth agape and hissing disapproval.

Vienna picked up paper and pencil and made a lightning sketch. But instead of reptilian features, she drew a swift caricature of the boss of Glenister. Bren Darcour's eyes and nose, his powerful jaw, even the deep lines that time and experience had etched on to his face—they were unmistakable.

The mouth, wide open and hissing disapproval, was his mouth . . .

Abby, coming out of the water, pounced on the sketch with gurgles of laughter.

'It's Uncle Bren! Oh, Vee, can I have it? Please— please——'

'No, you can't.' Hastily Vee turned the page, hiding her impulsive sketch. She was in enough bother without that drawing turning up to earn her a further dose of disapproval.

But the act of putting down on paper her hostility had somehow eased the tension. She sat contentedly sketching with Abby until the heat grew more intense, then she said, 'Lunch, I think, Abby.'

'Another minute.' Abby pored over her sketchpad, intent on what she was doing. 'I'm drawing your face, Vee, so I'll have something to remind me when I go back to school.'

Obediently Vienna posed until Abby progressed further with her portrait, then they walked slowly

back to the homestead. They had almost reached
the garden gate when Abby looked back and saw
the distant dust-swirl.

'Somebody's coming,' she announced, frowning
into the sunlight. 'And they're in a terrible hurry.
Look, Vee, how fast they're travelling.'

Vienna tipped the sunhat down over her eyebrows and stared into the shimmering distance.

Bren had planned to be home during the afternoon, but this was much too early. Nevertheless,
the dust resolved itself into the four-wheel-drive he
had taken out that morning.

Vienna and Abby stood and waited for it without speaking, because there was urgency in the way
it sped towards them. Abby swung the gate open,
and the Range Rover sped through without slow-
ing down. Bren was driving, and as he passed the
two girls he stared grimly ahead without acknow-
ledging the opened gate.

Vienna saw Neil hunched beside Bren, his face
glum and white, and apprehension crawled like
cold fingers under the thin skin of her confidence.

'Whatever have we done now?' she asked herself,
then wondered bitterly why she wasn't caring about
Neil, instead of developing guilt feelings before she
even knew what had happened.

The four-wheel-drive pulled up with a jerk at the
verandah. Neil's injuries couldn't be too serious.
He struggled up the verandah steps, one hand on
the rail, the other on Bren's shoulder; and he
managed a wan smile when Vienna and Abby
reached them.

Abby arrived first, because she had run like a
hare, but Vienna wasn't all that far behind her.
They stood staring helplessly while the master of
Glenister Two, grim-faced and implacable, helped

his guest on to the verandah. Neil's boot and sock had been removed from his left foot, and he stood at the top of the steps experimentally wriggling toes and instep and ankle. The movements didn't seem to be causing him too much pain, although the ankle was slightly swollen.

Abby asked curiously, 'What happened to you?' and because her voice was more censorious than sympathetic, Vienna interrupted quickly, 'If it's a sprained ankle we'll need ice, Abby. Why don't you go and get some?'

Colour was coming back into Neil's face, and once he muttered, 'Damned horse!' and avoided her eyes. Bren said nothing as he steered Neil along the verandah towards his bedroom. When they settled him on the bed he ordered curtly, 'I'll get bandages and dressings from the office. It looks only a minor wrench, but it needs attention. Abby's gone for ice, hasn't she?' He looked at Vienna, the lines between his nose and mouth graven deep and grim. 'I presume you can attend to it, if nothing's broken.'

'Of course I can.'

Bren didn't seem enormously relieved to find Neil's injuries only minor. He appeared thoroughly browned off by the whole happening.

Abby brought ice in a deep plastic bowl, and Vienna packed it around the ankle, while Abby watched anxious-eyed now, because there was tension in the atmosphere, and she felt it sharply.

When Bren came back with elastic bandages and cotton wool, he handed them silently to Abby; and when Neil winced as Vienna packed more ice around the swelling, the big man shot him a cold look from under those level eyebrows, a look that was almost contemptuous.

'You'd better have a drink,' he suggested. 'Abby, go get the brandy bottle, there's a good girl. Or whisky.'

'I'd rather have a Scotch.' Neil didn't bother to hide his resentment. Vienna saw the fingers of his left hand, where it rested on the bed cover, trembling spasmodically. Although his injuries didn't look serious, he'd had a shock. He was shaken and humiliated, and Brenden Darcour wasn't making him feel any better.

Neil muttered, 'That horse—that damned horse! He knows some dirty tricks,' and Bren said yes, but his lips scarcely moved.

'Got a damn nasty streak,' Neil elaborated. 'He ditched me deliberately. I'll swear he tried to slam me into the tree!'

The big man's features remained stone-carved. Abby came back with whisky and crushed ice and a glass, and Bren poured a drink. He handed it coolly to Neil, who sat on the edge of the bed now, ankle packed in ice, while Vienna unrolled bandages.

Afterwards, when the ankle was firmly strapped, Neil allowed himself to be made comfortable on the bed. Myra came to add her helping hand, her face drawn with dismay, but this time it was Vienna he wanted.

'I'm all right,' he brushed Myra off. 'Just got tossed by a nag with a dirty streak.'

Vienna picked up the basin of ice, to carry it away, and in the doorway she paused just long enough to stare haughtily at Bren. Her eyes were hot with anger.

'The horse isn't the only creature around here with a nasty streak,' she announced clearly.

'Now, I wonder what you could mean by that,

Nursie?' The granite face was dirt-streaked and grim, but his voice came softly, in a low drawl meant only for her.

Vienna raised her voice deliberately.

'You know darned well you forced Neil to ride an unruly horse!' She gestured bitterly towards Neil's bandaged ankle. 'I hope you're satisfied. That must make you feel really great. It's made your day, I'm sure.'

She stamped past him, and Abby followed her, skipping ahead to open the bathroom door. Anxious and pale-faced, she watched Vienna tip the melting ice out of the bowl, her troubled eyes following her every movement. When it was done, the bowl wiped and put away, she touched Vienna's sleeve tentatively.

She said in a small voice, 'Luci's back. She rode in while I fetched the whisky, and she brought Neil's horse back. She told me, Vee—about what happened. She said that wasn't the horse Neil was supposed to ride. He took another one instead, the big stallion Uncle Bren said he wasn't to handle.'

'Oh no!'

Vienna crumpled. She closed her eyes in dismay, and when she opened them Abby was staring at her with anguished eyes.

'You've gone white,' she wailed. 'I shouldn't have told you, should I?' Her mouth trembled. 'It's my fault. Like Luci says, I'm always doing stupid things.'

'No, you aren't. I—I'm truly grateful you told me. It's just that I feel such an utter idiot, rushing at your uncle like that. I'm the one who's acted like an idiot, Abby, not you.'

Vienna did her best to comfort Abby. She even tried to make a joke of it, telling the girl it was a good thing to happen, because now her uncle would rush off and get the car fixed and speed them on their way. But she wasn't fooling either of them.

Her heart was heavy, her spirits had taken a low dive into total dismay. Why must I be so impulsive? she asked herself over and over, while she set out salad lunches in the kitchen, and Abby hovered nearby, concerned and anxious.

When the lunches were arranged Vienna asked suddenly, 'Abby, can you look after everything for a couple of minutes? I'd better see your Uncle Bren, and apologise.'

'Do you have to?'

Vienna managed a bleak smile. 'Yes, I think I should.'

She went along the verandah and at the office door she hesitated, squared her shoulders, and knocked. Yes, he was there. His voice called 'Come in', and when Vienna opened the door he looked at her quietly, and to her astonishment his expression was almost reasonable. If anything, his mouth relaxed a little as he studied her, the corners slightly upturning, as if he might have been mildly amused. He motioned to one of the chairs alongside his desk, and when Vienna shook her head he looked at her quickly, his expression inscrutable.

'Oh, sit down, girl,' he ordered. 'I won't bite. Not today, anyway.'

Vienna felt more dignified standing, less susceptible to his authority. But he stared at her with those calm, commanding grey eyes, and she sat down weakly, because she hadn't yet rescued her morale from the terrible low it had plunged into after Abby's news.

She couldn't sit stiffly on the edge of the chair

for ever, so after a few more seconds she allowed herself to relax, and as she leaned back in the chair with a faint sigh, the big man took his attention away from her and walked to a small refrigerator in one corner of his office.

'Do you like your beer straight, or would you prefer a shandy?'

'Oh—a shandy, thanks.'

He opened the door and pulled out two bottles and two glasses that had been frosting on the shelves. Had he been expecting her? Of course not, she answered herself hastily. There was always the possibility of someone dropping in. Terry, or one of the stockmen. Or Luci . . .

She said carefully, 'I'm sure you know why I'm here, so I'd better—I'd better get on with it, hadn't I?'

She couldn't see his reaction. His fair head stayed bent over the lemonade he was adding to the beer in her glass. Then he looked quickly at her over his left shoulder, eyebrows quizzical.

'Well?'

'Well—what?'

'I thought you were planning to get on with it.'

Traitorous colour flooded her cheeks. She said stiffly, 'I came to apologise. I was rude—inexcusably rude——' He didn't contradict her. 'And—and I jumped to conclusions. In fact, I've made a complete ass of myself. I came to say I'm sorry, I apologise.'

His eyes held an expression she could not fathom. 'It doesn't suit you,' he said, after a small silence.

'What doesn't suit me?'

'Humility.' A faint smile tugged at his mouth. 'Those eyes were made for flashing.' He was laughing at her, but she couldn't respond.

He put the glass with her shandy within reach of her hand, but she couldn't pick it up, not yet.

She swallowed nervously. 'Will the horse——?' She left the rest of the sentence unspoken, because if the horse was injured, especially if it had to be destroyed, she didn't want to know about it, and yet in some dreadful way she had to find out.

Bren said swiftly, 'The horse is all right.' She thought he might have added, 'No thanks to Neil,' but he didn't. 'Poor Sister Maddern!' His voice was soft but mocking. 'You're having a rugged introduction to the outback, aren't you?'

Vienna moistened dry lips with her tongue.

'I expect you'll be glad to see us go.'

Outside his office window a jacaranda tree waved lacy fronds. Vienna watched it helplessly. Anything to avoid the hard scrutiny.

'Oh, I don't know.' His face remained enigmatic. 'Perhaps we needed something to shake us out of our apathy. You've certainly done that, haven't you?'

She stared at him suspiciously, waiting for some crushing comment, but he kept looking at her blandly, light from the window gleaming on his golden hair, eyebrows raised as though he might have challenged and then again he might not. As usual, his eyes remained impenetrable, revealing nothing of the thoughts behind them.

Vienna took a sip of her drink, then she said firmly, 'Well, I should like to apologise for any— for all the trouble we've caused. I hope Neil's car can be fixed soon and then—then we can go away back to Adelaide and leave you in peace to get on with your—your mustering, or whatever it is you should be doing, instead of having to rescue us.'

She swallowed. 'Neil's ankle isn't really bad. There's only a small amount of swelling. He says he'll be all right tomorrow, though I expect it'll take longer than that. But I can drive——'

Her voice trailed away. Bren wasn't looking in the least impressed.

'Are you sure you want to leave us in such a hurry, Miss Maddern?'

'Yes, I do—the sooner the better.'

'I thought you were anxious to get some outback experience, before you take over your own—um—estate.'

Vienna felt angry colour flood her face.

'I don't want your land,' she flashed. 'I never did want it.'

'You don't? Fancy that!' He put his glass down carefully on the desk. She watched his long strong fingers rearranging papers to make a clear space around the glass. His head remained bent, as if he concentrated on the papers, but suddenly he lifted it and scrutinised her carefully. The grey eyes were steel-cold, fiercely penetrating.

'I wonder then,' he questioned softly, 'I wonder why you should go to the trouble of travelling all this long way to look at something you don't want.'

Vienna stared at him dumbly. She couldn't say, 'I really don't know. I haven't the slightest idea why I allowed myself to be bundled away to look at some property I'd no intention of claiming . . . It just happened . . . I don't know how or why.' No, she couldn't . . . Nobody could admit to such an asinine thing, although it was true enough.

And she had no intention of offering some weak reason like, Perhaps I wanted to see the outback. He'd demolish that feeble excuse soon enough.

There had to be easier ways of getting yourself experience. He'd caught her without words.

'Well?' he prodded softly.

Vienna put her glass down on the desk with a snap.

'I don't have to explain my movements to you, Mr Darcour.'

His lips twisted. 'Mr Darcour? We're being formal, are we?'

Yes, we are, she told herself silently. And haven't you been formal all along? Miss Maddern this— Sister Maddern that—— But she wouldn't give him the satisfaction of letting him know she'd noticed. She'd had enough of arguing.

She said stiffly, 'That's an irrelevant question. I don't see how it can concern you.'

He went on musingly, as if she had not spoken. 'I hope you didn't do it for love of the young man who put that emerald on your finger. He seems rather fickle.' His expression remained quizzical, but his mouth was hard. 'You couldn't exactly call him devoted, could you? Only when he needs your tender loving care, I think.'

While she stared at him indignantly, with parted lips, he calmly picked up his glass and swallowed the rest of his drink. He was refilling his glass when he added softly, without changing expression, 'That leaves only me, doesn't it?'

Vienna stared at him in angry disbelief. She reached for her glass, sipped, and choked. 'If you mean what I think you mean—if you're suggesting I chased you up here——'

'Exhilarating thought, isn't it? For me, I mean. So intriguing. That a lovely young woman like yourself might pursue an ordinary fellow like me halfway across a continent——'

Vienna stood up abruptly. 'This conversation is becoming ridiculous!'

'Not ridiculous,' he contradicted. 'Untimely. I'll grant you that—it's untimely. You're not half as experienced as you'd like people to think, are you?'

'If you're suggesting——'

'If you're open to suggestions, I do have one.' He nodded towards Neil's engagement ring.

'Why don't you get rid of that—that encumbrance—from your finger, and then we might continue this discussion at a more appropriate time. It could open up all sorts of possibilities, don't you think? Who knows where it might lead us?' he added cryptically.

'It isn't going to lead anywhere.' Vienna straightened her shoulders defensively. She glowered at him.

'I came here to apologise——'

'And so you have, very handsomely. And I've accepted your apology, equally handsomely, I hope. Mind you,' his voice was soft, enigmatic, 'I won't guarantee not to claim compensation at some later date.'

Vienna pushed her chair with a clatter against the desk, setting glasses rattling.

'Well, you won't get it from me!' she snapped, and turned on her heel. As she stamped along the verandah she heard the soft mockery of his laughter; then he closed the door, and there was only the sound of her own heels on the wooden floor as she marched haughtily away.

She was still fuming as she walked into the kitchen.

'He's insufferable!'

Abby was taking dry biscuits out of a tin and arranging them on a platter, and Vienna set about beating cream cheese for a dip.

Abby studied her intently. 'You're better,' she announced. 'I'm so glad. I thought you might be going to faint or something. You looked terrible.' Her lip quivered. 'I kept wishing I hadn't said anything, about the horse, I mean.'

'I'm all right.'

Abby said tentatively, 'You told me not to let Uncle Bren spook me. How come you're so frightened of him?'

'I am not frightened.' The beater whirled in Vienna's hands.

Abby said cautiously, 'Anyhow, it's all over, isn't it?' and Vienna snapped, 'Of course it's all over,' as she sprinkled chopped chives into the dip. But it wasn't all over.

The big man had triumphed again . . . The autocratic man with the shining blond hair and the eyes that spoke of distance, he had teased her, nettled her, led her; watching her reactions as he might have handled a mettlesome colt. And he had stirred her, again . . . Even now her skin tingled because he had looked at her so intimately across his office desk, generating his power aura that threw her off balance whenever she got too close to him.

From now on, she would have to keep out of his way until Neil's car was repaired and they could leave. They would go back to Adelaide and forget all about this strange red land and the powerful men who mastered it.

In the meantime, all she had to do was keep cool. She spooned the dip into a white bowl with petalled edges, and put it in the centre of Abby's platter; then she drew a long steadying breath and remembered that she was not an impressionable teenager. She was a grown young woman who had finally encountered a man who shook her beyond anything she had ever known before, but surely she was capable of protecting herself.

She mightn't be as experienced as Bren Darcour, but she had learned control, and this was the time to exercise it.

She took the platter from Abby and carried it out to the verandah, where she arranged it on the centre of the table with steady hands.

CHAPTER SIX

NEIL insisted on hobbling out to the verandah for lunch, and because Bren and Luci were there too, it turned out a much more festive occasion than Vee had planned.

Bren seemed prepared now to overlook the 'borrowed' mount. He didn't mention it at all, and much of the restraint lifted.

Luci sat between the two men and divided her attention so skilfully that neither appeared slighted. Even Myra, satisfied that her beloved son was neither crippled nor in extreme agony, became almost skittish, making herself especially pleasant to Bren, entertaining them all with stories of her girlhood experiences on a 'finishing trip' to Europe many years ago. Her adventures had been unconventional, and Vienna wondered what had happened to Myra's adventurous spirit after she came back to Australia.

Afterwards heat invaded the verandah, seeping in blasts of warm air across the golden trumpets of allamanda and the white mandevilla flowers. Some trees hung their leaves, dispirited and wilting, and Jo-Jo had irrigation pipes seeping water over thirsty ground.

Dorothy's two Aboriginal girls, Noreen and Jenny, offered high-spirited help in the kitchen; and while they cleared away Vienna went outside to see whether Jo-Jo needed assistance in the garden. She wore fawn cotton slacks and a pale green shirt with long sleeves, and Bren insisted she call at the store for a hat that offered more protection than her navy cotton. He raised those cool eyebrows at her determination to go into the garden, advising her tersely that she must take advantage of whatever shade there might be, and not do anything strenuous.

'We managed before your arrival,' he pointed out coolly, 'and I daresay we'll manage after you go, so don't whip yourself until you collapse from heat exhaustion. It won't be appreciated.'

He thinks I'll get sunstroke and he'll have another patient on his hands, Vienna decided glumly, as she walked to the kitchen garden. And when Abby elected to leave her and join Luci and Bren at the pool, she wandered around the shade houses looking for Jo-Jo with an uncomfortable feeling of loneliness, as if she had been deprived of something.

It would have been easier to sit in the shelter of the summerhouse beside the pool. She could have taken a book from the homestead library and sat under the bougainvillaeas and browsed. But this could be her last chance to help Jo-Jo. It wasn't that she desired to keep out of the way of the bossman of Glenister Two. No, never ... She wouldn't allow him the satisfaction of admitting, even to herself, that all her good resolutions melted away as soon as she sat down at table with him. She had been just as much aware of him as ever; but she'd make very certain he didn't disturb her this afternoon.

She settled the broad-brimmed hat determinedly on her head and marched through the citrus trees to where Jo-Jo rattled tools in the workshop.

She said, 'I've come to help. Do you have any jobs you can delegate?' and he answered bluntly,

'Nope,' glaring at her out of those incredible bright eyes from under beetling brows, as if she had suddenly appeared from outer space.

'You must have. I mean, don't you want something done in the garden?'

'Nope.' Like a wise old gnome he peered at her. 'Go and have a swim,' he ordered gruffly, 'like everyone else—I can hear them from here, shouting and splashing. Why don't you go and play, too?'

'Because I don't want to. I—I wanted to help. I like growing things and I don't get much chance at home. Only pots and tubs, and not many of them, because I live in a flat.'

'Yeah. Well, there isn't much you can do in the heat of the day. Any idiot knows that.'

He darted quick flashing looks at her, wriggling his bushy brows frantically, and Vienna laughed in spite of his rebuff.

'Okay,' she admitted, 'so I don't know anything about gardening. But I would have liked to help. After all, you've rescued my poor sagebush.'

'Dunno about that. It's looking pretty sick. But at least it's not dead yet.'

He spoke gruffly, although the crinkled eyes had a lurking twinkle. Then he relented and let her work for about an hour in the shade houses, before he sent her away.

'Don't need you,' he announced firmly; and Vienna peeled off gardening gloves and went inside to don her swimsuit. The slim one-piecer revealed most of her figure, and she twisted in front of the mirror, trying to inspect her back. The bruises were fading, the scratches healing, but she would have to be careful to slide quickly into the water, and even then it might be risky. Better still, perhaps, she could cover up with a shirt, so that no one would see the telltale marks. She could easily make some excuse about dodging sunburn.

She brushed her thick black hair and plaited it high on her head, then rubbed sun filter cream over her face and limbs. As a last-minute extra, she picked up a striped wrap-around skirt and tied it deftly around her waist. For skin protection, she told herself; but she knew well enough she was erecting a barrier between her near-nakedness and the astute eyes of Glenister's master, should he glance her way.

He did look up as she approached the pool, saying nothing, watching her with glinting eyes as she walked towards him, his very silence expressing awareness, even derision. He knew Jo-Jo hadn't needed her.

He stood on the edge of the pool, one hand curved negligently on the end-rail, and because he had been swimming his skin shimmered with water, and the dancing light made small rainbows of every drop. No wonder he rode the mettlesome stallion so effortlessly! His hard tanned body looked efficient as an athlete's, and he stood there beside Luci, half smiling, half mocking, his body-hair gold-glistening in the sunlight, and all the bitterness and severity wiped from his features so that Vienna realised, with a faint sense of shock, that he was probably much younger than she had suspected. Not as young as she was, of course, probably in his mid-thirties; but certainly he had shed some years this afternoon.

Abby and Neil and Myra sat on deckchairs and recliners in the shaded summerhouse, while Bren and Luci joined Vienna in the pool.

Vienna wasn't sure that she wanted to swim with Bren. He gave her a piercing look when he saw she

was keeping the blouse on while she swam; and
Luci enquired slyly, 'Do you always swim fully
clothed, Vienna?' her eyes prickly and unfriendly,
so that Vienna's feeble excuse died on her lips, and
she dived into the water without any explanation
at all.

After the swim, as they sipped cool drinks under
the magenta-coloured flowers, Abby said, 'I want
to finish my drawing of you, Vee. Could you sit
for a while?' Vienna said uneasily yes, she could;
and Abby added brightly, 'I fetched your sketchbook, too, in case you want to work. What did
you do with it, Uncle Bren?'

Expression veiled, Bren reached beneath his deck-
chair and produced Vienna's sketchbook. She
accepted the book from him and dropped it on to
her lap while Abby tried to recapture the pose she
had begun yesterday.

Aware of Bren's attention as she turned her head
this way and that to please Abby, Vienna frowned
at him forbiddingly. She wished he'd go away and
swim again with Luci. As usual she found his nearness, and his cool attention, disturbing.

All too late, she remembered her sketch of the
frilled lizard. Of course he'd seen it, although not
by the flicker of an eyelid was he giving anything
away. She felt the rush of colour flooding her
cheeks while Bren leaned back in the chair, sipping
his drink and lazily watching her over the rim of
his glass, while Abby continued fidgeting.

Vienna prayed she didn't look nearly as embarrassed as she felt. What on earth must he be thinking of her lighthearted attempt to caricature? The
lizard prancing, frill expanded, mouth cavernous
and hissing—with his own unmistakable features!

If it made him angry, he was careful not to show

it. On the other hand, he most certainly wasn't amused either. The cool grey eyes remained remote, assessing her, impersonal as ever, while Abby frowned over her drawing. Suddenly she ripped the page out of her sketchbook, crumpled it, and dropped it crossly on to the ground.

'I'll have to start again. You look different this afternoon, Vee. I can't get the right angle, and your hair's done that new way.'

From the corners of her eyes, Vienna saw Bren pick up the crumpled sheet of paper. He smoothed it out, and after studying it for a few moments folded it into his towel.

Abby said severely, 'It's not finished, Uncle Bren. I can do better than that, truly I can.'

'I'm sure you can,' his voice was silky, 'but I'll have it, just the same.' As Vienna began wondering why he would rescue a drawing of her face, and a crumpled one at that, he added calmly, 'When you're famous, young lady, I might be able to sell it for a fortune. An original Abigail Darcour. One of her first.'

So it wasn't for the subject he had rescued the picture; he was making that plain enough. Though it certainly wouldn't make him a fortune. Perhaps he wanted to study it quietly, in order to decide whether his niece had talent.

Vienna turned her back on him, and made a new pose for Abby, and very soon he and Luci and the others wandered back to the homestead.

Much later, back inside after Abby had completed her sketch, Vienna re-bandaged Neil's ankle. He had been fortunate, it seemed; the swelling was almost gone, and there appeared no ill effects.

Neil said ruefully, 'I guess it's true what they say: every duck to his own pond. I'm certainly not

winning many points up here, am I? Can't seem to
take a trick.'

'I wouldn't worry,' Vienna lied. She was fretting
enough for all three of them, but it wouldn't do
any good to let Neil guess how shattered she was.

Deftly she replaced the bandage, and Neil peered
down at it from his position on the bed.

'How's it look?'

'Not much swelling left. You should be all right
tomorrow—fortunately.'

Neil grinned, shamefaced. 'Whatever would I do
without you?'

Vienna answered, 'You'd do very well,' and was
astonished by her own reaction. That wasn't what
she had intended saying. She ought to have
produced some lighthearted comment like 'Glad to
be of use,' or 'It's nice to be needed'—but her
tongue had uttered that flat statement. 'You'd do
very well.'

She sighed. He probably would, at that. All her
feelings were jumbled in unfamiliar patterns. She
didn't understand herself any more. She wondered
whether she ever would again. More than anything,
she had wanted Neil to feel a need of her. How
much time had she spent letting herself dream
about having the right to care for him, to share
experiences, maybe even the whole future . . .

Now here they were, she the nurse, he the
patient, and it was exactly as it always was with
her other patients—a feeling of compassion and a
desire to ease discomfort, that was all.

How could feelings change so suddenly?
Something had gone wrong with their relationship,
leaving her disorganised and unsure of herself.
Maybe she would feel a revival of the old attraction
when they got back to Adelaide. Or hadn't it been

strong enough in the first place to face the pressures of changed situations?

Neil didn't seem to need her either, once he was reassured about the jarred ankle. He and Luci drove down to the Aborigines' camp later while Bren went back to the muster; and there was nothing said about Vienna joining them to choose souvenirs.

They came back with digging baskets, a boom-erang and some body shields. They had several carved and decorated wooden lizards. Neil pre-sented Vienna rather guiltily with a necklace made out of pea-shaped seeds. They were the usual desert colours, red and orange and brown and cream, and Vienna put them carefully away. Some day they might be all she had left of her outback adventure.

She took a lot of care over her dressing that even-ing. A defence mechanism, she decided. The more confused her feelings, the more desperately she needed the morale-booster of knowing she looked unruffled.

She chose an emerald-green jersey dress, very plain except for tiny draped sleeves that extended into a cross-over bodice that outlined her breasts and diminished her waistline, so that she appeared even slimmer—and fancier, she hoped—than usual. The dress, cut fairly high at the back, neatly covered what remained of her bruises.

She reached for the cream shoes she'd worn with her suit on the evening of her skirmish in the garden with Bren. Somehow, somewhere, during that confrontation the heel of one shoe had split. It hung askew and there was no chance of repair. The only other shoes in her wardrobe that might do were the red-strapped sandals she had worn on

her first day. She put them on, then impulsively
she yielded this time to temptation, and clipped a
couple of frangipanni flowers into the wings of her
glossy hair.

In the kitchen the two Aboriginal girls, Noreen
and Jenny, were already busy. They smiled at
Vienna with happy faces, offering goodwill from
brown velvet eyes, and their footsteps on the tiled
floor were light as dry saltbush blowing on the
wind.

Vienna enveloped herself in one of Dorothy's
large bright aprons; and when Bren came in to get
cold beer from the fridge he said, 'Under that tent
you're wearing, I'm positive you look very splendid
this evening, Miss Maddern. Is it a special occasion?' and she shook her head.

'No. Except that we can't have many more
evenings to put in before we set out for home.
Neil's ankle is mending quickly. No doubt your
mechanic will be free any day now. I expect
you'll be as pleased to get rid of us as we are to
go.'

Bren stood there with the cold beer cans in his
strong brown hands. He wore tailored maroon
slacks and an open-necked cream silk shirt, and
the light shone down on his gold-and-silver hair,
as it always did, and his teeth flashed white as he
let his sensuous lips curl in a mocking half-smile.

And quite suddenly, as if someone had flung a
blazing light into the room, Vienna had the answer
to the question she had asked herself that afternoon
while she bandaged Neil's ankle. How could a
genuine attraction between two people suddenly
disappear as if it had never existed? She knew
now . . . Because a stronger feeling for someone else
had taken its place. Because illusion cannot stand

up to reality . . . Because the sun will blot out the moon . . .

The man with the grey eyes was looking at her across the room with the quizzical expression that could have meant anything, or nothing at all. It smoothed away harshness, so that strain-lines were erased, and grimness eased into possible friend-liness . . . because he was smiling . . . really smiling, with warm companionship.

'Don't tell me you'll be glad to leave us, Miss Maddern. We'll miss you.'

He was baiting her, of course. She turned away, shaken, concealing herself from his probing. There was no way she could ever let those shrewd, level eyes guess at the disastrous truth.

She had fallen in love for ever with the master of Glenister Two. As simply as that. She was in-curably, deeply in love with a man who had never tried to conceal his dislike and disapproval since their first meeting . . . attracted to him as she had never been drawn to another human being. And it wasn't fair. Because there was no way she could untangle herself from the trap, no one to care or even notice that she had walked into it.

She allowed herself time for a long steadying breath before she turned and faced him. When she spoke her voice was as cool as his. 'Hadn't you better get on with your duties? Dinner is almost ready.' Nobody would have guessed how hard it was to face him calmly across the kitchen benches, chin tilted, eyes controlled.

He paused in the doorway. 'Come and have a drink with us. Noreen can serve dinner without you.'

He flashed Noreen an encouraging smile. Vienna thought, Of course Noreen will serve dinner.

Without a protest. After that look, Noreen would probably die for you, and so would I. Only I won't let you know it.

She lingered to add the final touch of a sprinkling of Jo-Jo's fresh parsley over the casserole, and when she looked around again the big man still lounged in the doorway, and under his arm, snuggled like a coaxing kitten, Luci purred. You could practically hear her purring across the room, Vienna decided crossly.

Bren inclined his head to talk to Luci.

'Come to help out, have you?' he teased, and Luci pouted deliciously before she said, not without a sharp edge to her honey-sweet voice,

'No, I haven't. It's just as well we're not all busybodies, or there'd be no room to move in the kitchen at all, would there?'

Luci looked dreamy in a splashy chiffon sheath that clung more than it floated, and yet managed to look ephemeral and seductive, and well Luci knew it. She vibrated sensuality. She came alive with it every time the master of Glenister Two came within reaching distance of her charms.

She said archly, 'Darling, you owe me a walk in the garden tonight, remember? You promised to show me the moon on the flowers before I went home.'

The big man's expression became indulgent.

'Not tonight, I'm afraid, Luci. I have to see Terry about repairing Neil's car at Red Vistas, now we have the bores under control. The moon and flowers will have to keep, I'm afraid.'

Vienna knew he had noticed the flowers in her hair; his glance slid smoothly over her again before he ushered Luci neatly out the doorway.

'Don't forget the drinks,' he reminded Vienna,

glancing over his right shoulder as he shut the door.

Vienna thrust plates furiously on to the warmer.

'Busybodies,' Luci had said, dripping honey and venom; and he hadn't bothered to contradict her. Vienna's well-meant efforts at helping, to try and relieve the strain of three extra visitors, were certainly not being accepted in the spirit in which they were offered. Busybodies. What was it Neil had said? Every duck to his own pond!

Neil wasn't the only one who couldn't do anything right in the unfamiliar environment, she reflected ruefully.

She counted out the last dinner plate, took off the apron, and left the kitchen to Noreen and Jenny. A mirror in the hallway told her that her cheeks were flushed, whether from the heat of the kitchen or the heat of her own feelings, she didn't waste time trying to decide.

Bren was behind the bar, dispensing drinks.

'What would you like, Miss Maddern? Beer or spirits?'

'Oh,' she stared at him helplessly, 'I don't know. Anything.' Coolness had deserted her, she stammered like a tongue-tied schoolgirl.

'Brandy, lime and soda,' he decided tranquilly. 'Brandy for your wellbeing. The other ingredients will cool you down.'

She marched across the room to the bar.

'What makes you think I need cooling?'

The grey eyes, not so much frosty now as tinged with a hint of searching mockery, surveyed her deliberately, from the black hair with its pink-tinged frangipanni, to the incongruous red shoes.

'It's been a warm day,' he commented enigmatically. The remark seemed not without significance, but she shied away from it hurriedly, pro-

ducing a cool smile to protect herself from the
potency of his nearness.

I am not a juvenile, she reminded herself grimly.
I am a fully grown young woman. And I have just
fallen in love, simply but dramatically, with a man
I hardly know. So how do I get myself out of this
little predicament?

Luci came and joined them at the bar, but it
didn't make any difference. Vienna remained
drowningly aware of him, and she stayed that way
throughout the meal ... aware of the movements
of his hands, the timbre of his voice, always cool
and calm, even judgemental, as if he weighed
everything he said and was conscious of its value;
knowing he spoke with authority even if it were
only discussing Luci's intentions to make Jo-Jo
plant orchids in the summerhouse under the bougainvillaeas.

Jo-Jo would plant whatever he wanted, and Bren
was explaining to Luci how she ought to know he
never interfered with his gardener's activities, for
fear he might have to deal with the job himself,
which he didn't want to do ...

And Vienna thought, looking at Luci, 'Ha!
Who's being a busybody now?' while Bren's level
eyes looked at her down the length of the table.
Not by the slightest flicker of expression did he
show that he read her thought and understood it
perfectly; but Vienna was perfectly sure he did.
Their glances linked, as if suddenly they shared that
one flash of intuition together, before he returned
his attention to Luci and her blandishments.

Vienna was astonished to find her hands shaking. She who had always taken pride in calmness
and control, was trembling with emotion.
Unobtrusively, she rested her knife and fork on

her plate, and left them there until she knew she had her feelings well under control. There were too many sharp eyes around the table. Whatever these mad feelings were she had developed towards Bren Darcour, they were harmless so long as nobody else suspected them.

After dinner, when Noreen and Jenny insisted they could do without her in the kitchen, Vienna went restlessly to her room.

She took the flowers out of her hair and put them back in the vase. That had been a foolish thing to do, dressing up like a girl on her first date, just because the frangipanni were velvet-smooth and fragrant and she had this wild idea of prettying herself up . . . as if she and Luci were conducting a contest, and she didn't want to admit defeat without making a final colourful gesture. Like sinking with your flag nailed to the mast—she grimaced at her reflection in the mirror, before going back to the sitting room to ask whether Neil's ankle needed attention after his excursion.

But Neil didn't want to be disturbed. He and Myra and Luci were playing cards, and when they invited Vienna to join them Bren said equably, 'No, she can't. Not tonight. She's to come with me to make arrangements with Terry about repairing the car. It's no use Neil hobbling down to Terry's place. He's used that ankle enough today.' He turned to Vienna. 'You can handle it, can't you?'

She nodded dumbly. 'I suppose so.'

There was nothing to handle, as far as she could see. All she had to do was hand over the keys of the car, and she could do that just as well at the homestead as down at Dorothy and Terry's bungalow.

Neil mumbled, 'My ankle's all right,' but he

made no effort to get up from the card table. Luci shot Vienna a murderous glare, and Abby jumped up from the pile of records she was examining, and pleaded, 'Can I come too, Uncle Bren? I want to see Dorothy about some—about something.'

'About whether she'd like some of your sketches for her Christmas cards, perhaps?'

Bren's voice was carefully smooth, but his mouth-corners twitched. Abby didn't have anything special to see Dorothy Green about, but she was lonely. She didn't want to be left at the homestead with only the card-players for company.

It may not have been exactly what he had planned, but Bren Darcour obviously decided to be philosophical about the rearrangement of his plans. He sent both girls away for jackets or cardigans, and again glancing at the red shoes, suggested Vienna change into something more stalwart.

Later, as they ambled through the citrus grove towards Terry's house, he asked questions about how Abby was getting on with her sketching and how she planned to go about getting herself accepted at art school when her secondary education was finished.

'Miss Hilda will help me. She's our art teacher at school, and she's really great. She says I have talent, and—and I ought to be a book illustrator, if that's what I truly want to do.'

Abby was still rather nervous of her uncle, and the words came out in a breathless rush, but after a while, as they walked through the warm velvet night, she breathed more easily and chattered freely until they reached Terry's house.

Vienna wondered what she and Bren might have talked about if Abby had not been there. Although in the evenings he let himself be drawn into Luci's flirtations, Bren Darcour was basically a reticent man—not inarticulate, just private, as though he withheld some part of himself always in reserve.

Yet Vienna was to discover that in Terry's home he chatted as easily as if he had borrowed Abby's tongue. Terry had discovered a waterhole drying up and another threatened by sand drifts. In the worksheds behind the Glenister homestead, Vienna had noticed a grader as well as the utility and Range Rover; and listening to the men she realised that there were some parts of this country that were continually changing. Just as the light pouring over it at sunrise and sunset wrought dramatic colour-illusions, so did the other forces of nature—wind and rain and dust-storms—change shapes and contours so that in some places the only permanent features seemed to be the harsh and stubborn rocks.

For a while, the adults sat in Dorothy's lounge room drinking cold beer, while Dorothy produced lemonade for Abby. Dorothy had spent the day baking, and the delicious fragrance of new-made bread still wafted from the kitchen.

Dorothy had chosen her husband in the image of her father. The resemblance was startling, Like Jo-Jo, Terry Green was a wiry, quick-moving small man, with an alert dark face and a thatch of curly dark hair that would some day be grizzled black and silver, like his father-in-law's.

Both Bren and Terry wore light-coloured shirts, open-necked, and the tanned skin of face and limbs threw their bodies into strong relief against Dorothy's yellow walls.

Her children—Joanne, Mary and young Joe—pored over their homework for school. When they

had finished, they collected their books and moved
into the lounge; and the adults went into the well-
lit kitchen, where Terry spread out maps and paddock charts over the table under the bright light.
The men spent more than an hour discussing bores
and fences. They were so engrossed that Vienna
wondered whether they were even aware the
women were in the room at all. But almost as if he
had some special receiver that picked up her thinking, the fair-haired man turned his head slightly
and raised his fine eyebrows and smiled at her.

'We'll get around to your car in a while,' he
promised quietly. As if he thought she might be
anxious not to waste time before he and Terry got
on to the job of repairing Neil's car, so that she
could get away from Glenister as soon as possible.

Dorothy said warmly, 'Don't hurry, Bren. I can
do with Vienna's company for as long as she'll stay.
Sometimes I wonder how we managed without
her,' and it seemed to Vienna that the big man
became unaccountably withdrawn as he returned
his attention to the charts. He didn't intend having
her around too long, that was for sure. Why then
had he dragged her down here to listen to a discussion in which she had no part?

She wondered whether he intended that she
should travel with them tomorrow and take the
responsibility of driving Neil's car back to
Glenister. She hoped not. She found the idea of
driving solo in that vast countryside strangely
daunting. With someone beside her—yes, she
wouldn't mind that at all. But alone, tackling sand-
drifts and cattle grids, she didn't fancy it at all.
There had been sections on the highway where
constant grading had shaved the road surface so
low that walls of sand towered on either side. She

didn't like those stretches at all, the high sand blotting out the countryside until she had found herself thinking, What if the whistling wind turned sour and the sand began to move? What then?

But if the boss-man decreed that she must drive Neil's car, then she would have to do it. You didn't argue with Bren Darcour, not if you valued your peace of mind. So she would do what he wanted, although she found the prospect quite terrifying.

Apprehensively, she stole a swift look across the table, and he was gazing at her, grey eyes gleaming and those usually grim lips soft-curved in a half-question, as if he might have been wondering what made her send that anxious signal in his direction.

Flustered, she turned away quickly to speak to Dorothy, trying to shut herself away from the sound of the men's voices. Just as she expected, arrangements for the trip to Red Vistas the following day took only a few minutes. Terry had located whatever they might need in case the axle was damaged; they settled on tools and equipment. It was decided the men should leave well before daybreak, allowing two to three hours' drive each way, and a couple of hours to do the repairs. Bren and Terry would travel together in the utility. There was no mention of Vienna going with them.

When Dorothy offered, 'Who's for scones and tea?' Vienna expected Bren to refuse politely and make his way homeward, but he didn't. They moved back to the lounge and settled back contentedly for more talking, while Abby joyfully helped Dorothy's children butter scones and cut cake while Dorothy made tea.

It was quite late when Bren pushed back his chair. 'If we're leaving before daybreak tomorrow I suppose we'd better get some sleep.' He tweaked

Abby's hair playfully. 'And so had you, young Abby, if you plan to get your imagination to work and produce a masterpiece before you go back to school.'

Abby looked at him reproachfully. 'Uncle Bren, you know it'll be at least another year before I can produce masterpieces!' and he tilted back his head and roared with laughter.

Because his laughter was so rich and rare, Abby laughed with him, although she wasn't sure really whether she oughtn't to have been offended. She glanced doubtfully at Vienna.

They were standing ready to move out of the comfortable lounge, and Dorothy was stacking cups and saucers on to a tray, when she said, 'Vienna, if my grandmother were here—which she's not, God rest her soul—she'd advise you to be very careful what you do tomorrow.' Smiling, she turned Vienna's cup slowly in her hand. 'There's lightning in your cup,' she said.

Terry laughed. 'Don't take any notice, Vee. It's witchcraft.'

'Lightning—what does that mean?'

Dorothy chuckled. 'According to my dear departed grandmother, a streak of lightning in your tea-leaves means you're in danger for the next twenty-four hours. You must walk with your eyes wide open wherever you go. I don't know how you are about tea-leaves, but my old grandma consulted her tea-cup every morning before she made a move.'

'Your grandmother,' Terry announced severely, 'was an over-imaginative, superstitious old lady. Didn't you tell me once she bruised both her knees trying to dodge a ladder?'

'I know,' Dorothy admitted. 'But it was the tea-leaves she really relied on, not dodging ladders.'

Bren took the cup from her hand and looked into it curiously, half smiling.

'Show me,' he demanded.

'There, see?' The zigzag of brown leaves stretched from the rim of the cup to its base.

'That could be anything,' Terry scoffed, peering around Bren's crooked elbow.

Dorothy pushed the cup towards him. 'Such as? Go on, tell us.'

'Ah, well, let's see. A bit of bent wire. An off-course boomerang after it's hit a tree——'

'It's lightning.' Dorothy took the cup from Bren's hand. 'Indisputably lightning,' she announced. 'And my grandmother always said——' she lowered her voice in mock-dramatics—'walk with your eyes wide open all day tomorrow.'

'I wish you hadn't seen that,' Abby shivered. 'It's scarey, and I don't like it a bit.'

'Oh, Abby!' Remorsefully, Dorothy swirled the dregs in Vienna's cup until the streak disappeared. 'It's only a joke, Abby,' she explained. 'There, it's gone. Anyway, reading tea-leaves went out of fashion decades ago. It was just a game people played when they had nothing better to do. My grandmother did it to pass the time away. Nobody really believes tea-leaves can tell you anything.'

Abby slipped her hand into Vienna's, and tugged.

'I guess not,' she admitted. 'Still, I'm glad there aren't any storms around, so you won't get struck by lightning tomorrow.'

'Not likely to be,' Terry grinned. 'The nearest thunderbolt is miles away, and likely to stay there. Don't worry, young Abby, the only storm we'll have around here is in that tea-cup. And there won't be any more,' he chuckled, 'because from now on we're buying tea-bags.'

'Or a tea-strainer.' Dorothy offered Abby a cheerful smile. 'Meanwhile, how about collecting some fresh bread for Vienna from the kitchen. How much can you carry?'

Abby came back from the kitchen with two armfuls of fresh bread and buns, all of which she insisted on carrying herself.

'This is so peaceful,' Vienna murmured blissfully, as they walked back to the house. 'I listened one night and I couldn't hear a single sound—no traffic, no people, except us. Not a whisper.'

'Except the generator,' Abby contradicted. 'You can hear that, can't you? It's always there.'

'I forgot it. Isn't that odd? I suppose you get so used to some sounds you don't even notice them.'

'Most people do, after a while.' Bren's voice was a mystery in semi-darkness.

'I suppose it's like listening to your own heartbeats. You don't even notice.'

'You have a nice way of putting things, Sister Maddern. Listening to your own heartbeats,' Bren's voice teased out of the shadows. 'Was that your professional training speaking, or are you beginning to be seduced by the enchantment of the Australian outback?'

Vienna made herself busy assisting Abby with the load of bread.

'I don't know.'

The truth was, she didn't want to know. And she didn't want to be seduced by anybody or anything. She wanted to go to Adelaide, she reminded herself silently, and forget Glenister Two and the catastrophe of Red Vistas as fast as ever she could.

If the car was repaired tomorrow, surely they

could leave next day, and she would start forgetting the man with distant eyes. He had charisma, and she was reacting in a totally immature way. Even now, walking beside him through the citrus grove, she knew that if Abby had not been there, and he had reached out for her from the shadows where he walked, she would have been powerless to run away. She was trapped by her own responses, controlled by feelings instead of reason. And the longer she stayed the worse it would get.

The moon silvered worksheds and store and the long corridors between lemon and orange trees. Despite Vienna's fears, Bren didn't mention the journey to Red Vistas; didn't invite her to go with him tomorrow for a last look at the wreck of Evelyn Harryn's dreaming.

Nor, fortunately, did he suggest she might drive Neil's car home. That must be Terry's job, and Vienna was thankful.

As they climbed the verandah steps Bren asked, 'What are your plans for tomorrow, Miss Maddern?' and Vienna said she had none at all, unless Neil wanted to visit the Aboriginal camp again for more artefacts. She would have appreciated seeing the craftsmen at work; but if not then she would have a restful day.

Abby was to go for an early-morning ride with Luci. Luci had insisted upon it. Her duty, she made it clear, was to prepare her niece for life in the outback, and riding expertly was one of the things she must learn to do before she was accepted by her uncle.

Luci had half-heartedly included Vienna in the invitation, but Vienna knew there was no way she could keep up with Luci and Abby, and Luci didn't press.

Luci rode beautifully. She had the outback

woman's knack of sitting a horse so that the
movements of horse and rider harmonised, and
Vienna always watched Luci enviously when she
rode. Luci she did not like; but Luci on a horse
was really something to see. She obviously had
equipped herself to fit perfectly into both worlds—
the city and the outback, and it would be churlish
to deny her the achievement. Vienna only wished it
didn't make her feel so inadequate.

At the top of the steps Abby hurried off to the
kitchen with her new bread. Bren and Vienna
walked along the verandah and as they paused
outside her room, he asked abruptly, 'What was it
Dorothy told you to do tomorrow? Walk with your
eyes wide open, wasn't it?'

Vienna found the courage to lift her eyes saucily
to his in the half-light.

'I always do,' she told him pertly.

'You surprise me.' His voice was cryptic. 'I could
have sworn you didn't always stop to work out
what you are doing.' He added smoothly, 'I don't
think we'll be too long fixing the car tomorrow.
It's just a matter of getting down there with the
right tools. With a bit of luck we should be back
about mid-afternoon.'

Vienna said carefully, 'We've caused you a lot of
trouble. I'm sorry.'

His smile was, as usual, a flash of white in the
darkness.

'If you think that's a lot of trouble,' he was using
his indulgent voice, the one he generally kept for
Luci, 'then you don't know much about the
Outback. We can contend with fire and floods,
droughts and even the occasional tornado. So don't
worry yourself unduly, Miss Maddern, about any
inconvenience you may have caused us.'

She expected him to move away, but he stayed there, leaning lazily against the door frame.

'I had a kitten like you once.' His lips curved in the soft smile that turned her heart. 'His name was Timmy—black fur, green eyes, pink tongue. I was very fond of him when I was six years old.'

Now he was laughing. Vienna compressed her lips, and her eyes flashed fire.

'What did you do with him?' she scoffed. 'Mince him up for hamburgers?'

He laughed. 'You don't find us very sympathetic, do you? Never mind ... one of these days,' he stretched out a long arm to open her door, so close she felt the brushing of his sleeve over her shoulder, 'one of these days we may surprise you.'

'Don't count on it.'

Surprisingly, unexpectedly, he leaned down and planted a swift goodnight kiss on her half-parted lips. A cool kiss, friendly and firm, his mouth not longering long enough to light up any fires. Just the sweet, fleeting pressure, the smell of after-shave, and the warmth of his curved fingers trailing from the nape of her neck to the hollow of her throat.

Then he withdrew. Deliberately, he broke contact, as if he might have decided there were other things that needed his attention.

Vienna waited dazedly for him, after amusing himself in that brief lighthearted moment, to turn and stride away. But he stayed there, looking down at her, and she heard the soft sound of his breathing. Then he bent again, resting a warm cheek against her hair for one fleeting moment.

'Don't forget,' he said, 'walk with your eyes wide open tomorrow. We wouldn't want anything to happen to you, would we?'

Then he was gone.

CHAPTER SEVEN

BREN and Terry left early next morning, long
before daybreak. The moon had vanished but stars
were still crisp in the sky when twin shafts of light
swung over the blackness outside Vienna's window.
Headlights.

Without knowing it, she had been watching for
them, waiting for the merest sound to tell her the
big man was on his way. The knowledge made her
furious with herself. How could she have become
so attuned to a man that she needed to know his every
movement? Here she was, lying in bed, like a schoolgirl anxious about her first crush. Listening. Needing
to be aware whether he moved this way or that,
how far apart they were going to be today; imagin-
ing how he would look as he and Terry bent over
the mangled car, straightening twisted bodywork.

Here was a man not likely to spare her a second
thought, unless he had a whim to amuse himself
for an hour or two.

Luci—Bren—they suited each other. That pair
belonged together like saddles and horses, like
birds and waterholes, exciting man and super-
polished woman . . .

You could become a casualty pretty quickly,
getting involved with a man like Bren Darcour. So
slow down, Vienna advised herself. Do some steady
breathing, do deep thinking . . . Lull yourself back
to sleep. And somehow she did it. She curled herself
up in bed and slowly, by design, coaxed herself
back to sleep.

Next time she awoke there were birds raucous in

the garden trees, squabbling over territories among the branches. She got up and dressed swiftly for breakfast.

Luci had Abby attired in jeans and denim shirt, with her hair in two tight plaits, drawn back severely from her sharp little face, so that her grey eyes shone large and wary and vulnerable, not at all like her Uncle Bren's. She was resigned to spending the next several hours riding, but managed to convey by her lost and solemn expression that she didn't expect to enjoy it.

After breakfast she hovered a little, offering to help Vienna and the girls in the house, but Luci whisked her off smartly.

Noreen and Jenny were away tidying rooms, and Vienna was stacking the last dishes away when Neil appeared in the kitchen.

'Can you cut sandwiches or something? We're going on a trip. Hurry up, Vee!'

She stared at him, bewildered. 'Who's going on a trip?'

'We are.' He looked around the kitchen impatiently. 'Who does that stuff when we're not here? Can't somebody else do it this morning?'

'No. Dorothy has three young children doing schooling. She has to supervise. And I just sent Noreen and Jenny off to do the house. The least I can do is clear up after breakfast.'

'Can you hurry it up a bit, then. Cut some sandwiches or something, in case we need a meal.'

'Neil, whatever for?' she protested.

'We're going treasure-hunting.' He said it importantly, as if he might be announcing a trip to Buckingham Palace. 'I've told that old fellow—the one that does the gardening——'

'Jo-Jo.'

'If that's his name, yes.'

'Who's going? You and Myra?'

Neil didn't try to curb his impatience. He said, 'Oh, for pity's sake, stow it, Vee! How could Mother go treasure-hunting in the desert? You know she can't——'

She looked at him levelly. 'Nobody's going treasure-hunting in the desert,' she said clearly.

Neil wasn't limping this morning, though he still wore the bandage. He'd done the strapping himself. When he saw that Vienna wasn't impressed by his request, he held out his left hand suddenly, thrusting it towards her, and in his palm she saw several pieces of rock. Not very large, and not exciting. She studied them dubiously.

'What are they supposed to be? Relics from Lassiter's Gold Reef?'

'Oh, don't be daft, Vee!'

He didn't like being put down. Not much had happened to sustain his pride since they'd left Adelaide; and now he was consumed with a kind of eagerness that vitalised his handsome face, and put an eager gleam into his eyes.

Neil excited and happy gave out a kind of persuasive energy she had always found endearing. Vienna looked at him now, feeling guilty because she could not share his enthusiasm.

'Neil, the desert is miles away——'

He shook his head.

'Not this one. Not the fringe, anyway, where the old diggings are. It's a fair distance, of course, but we can get there and back before the men get home from Red Vistas. I know—I worked it out. And I'll pay for the fuel, Vee. It's not stealing——'

'Neil, I don't know what you're talking about,

but I won't go wandering in the desert in the heat.
We could finish up with sunstroke, or worse.
Snakes—taipans——'

His voice became scathing.

'There are no taipans in central Australia.
They're all up north. Honestly, Vee——'

'We'd probably find worse things. We don't
know anything about the desert, Neil.'

With a finger of his right hand Neil sorted the
pieces of rock in his left palm.

'See these? I got them from a couple of
Aborigines at the camp yesterday. Look—honey
opal—clear smoky quartz—coloured quartz—
They're not diamonds or sapphires, I admit, but
they'd be something we found for ourselves, real
souvenirs. There are these old diggings. I know
exactly where to find them, just a little way into
the desert. So we won't make our fortunes! What
does that matter? We'll take back something extra
special to show everybody.'

Vienna protested, 'You have the artefacts you
bought yesterday.'

His jaw hardened. 'This is different. I want
something I got for myself. I know the exact position—there's a humpbacked mountain to use as
marker. We can't get lost.'

She hated to quench his enthusiasm. He wasn't
going to like it at all, but there was no way she
could allow herself to sneak off into the desert to
look for gemstones while the master of Glenister
Two was away fixing their car.

She looked at him across the kitchen benches.

'No,' she said.

The handsome jaw set stubbornly.

'It isn't much to ask.'

'I know you don't think it is. But I can't do it,

Neil. I honestly can't.'

'I'm not persuading you to do anything illegal. All I want is that you cut a few sandwiches to keep us going in case we're late for lunch. I've borrowed the Range Rover. The old guy in the garden knows I'm taking it. I've checked fuel, oil, water. We'll even carry spare petrol—I'm not stupid.'

Vienna tried again. 'You didn't ask Bren. You think we can just help outselves to the man's Range Rover? Suppose he comes back to find his four-wheel-drive missing, and us with it? What kind of guests will he think we are?'

'I told you, I've explained it all to the fellow, Jo-Jo.' But he wasn't looking her straight in the eye. She thought, I wonder exactly what you told Jo-Jo; whether you let him think you have Bren's permission. Then she steeled herself.

'No,' she said again.

'Then I'll go alone.' Neil was angry; his lips curled scornfully. 'Just give me some food and drink, for heaven's sake. That isn't too much to ask, is it? That you should provide a man with something to eat?'

'All right.'

Her hands, holding the knife, shook as she cut into Dorothy's fresh bread. She didn't know why. But she had expected the day to pass quietly, now here was Neil with rash plans for a journey into the desert in search of souvenirs, anything to patch his damaged pride.

Vienna didn't know anything about old diggings, but surely if they were abandoned it must mean they no longer yielded anything of value. The desert lay west of Glenister Two's boundary, marked by a range of blue-purple rocky mountains that sometimes turned harsh red in a sunset, and on other days became invisible. Swathed in shimmering haze, they floated away into nothingness, reappearing only when clarity came down over the land, bringing everything nearer and clearer. The sight of Red Vistas, dusty and crumbling, had given Vienna a distaste for deserts. They were places of harsh rocks and lonely wind and destructive creeping sand. They were places that killed dreams.

Reluctantly, she made Neil's sandwiches and packed buns and a thermos of tea, then added an ice-cold drink in an extra flask.

She found herself wondering whether she and Neil would ever again be able to work harmoniously together, and decided it didn't matter. There were other hospitals and nursing homes, or Dr Jason would accept her back specialling.

She carried her packages on to the verandah for Neil to collect; when she had arranged them she looked up, and Myra was standing there, watching her. Myra wore a blue silk dressing-gown, with a hairnet over her carefully-tended lavender waves, and her eyes were accusing.

She said bluntly, 'You're letting him go alone, are you?' as if Vienna had deserted her son. Vienna knew that it probably looked that way to Neil's mother, as if she'd deserted him.

She said quietly, 'He doesn't have to go,' and to her horror Myra nodded agreement and Vienna saw that she couldn't speak because her lips were shaking.

Myra being pretentious and over-protective, even incurably snobbish, Vienna could deal with. She could even get a little amusement out of it. But Myra with her eyes scared and watery, her elegant fingers clutching and unclutching the blue silk gown until it bunched in her hands, made her feel guilty.

Myra took a tiny lace handkerchief from her pocket and delicately dabbed at her eyes, and when she spoke she sounded very unlike the poised Myra who had left Adelaide not long ago.

She mumbled huskily, 'He's very impulsive. He always has been,' and when Vienna said 'Yes,' she added pathetically, 'It's his leg I'm worried about. His ankle. If he's hurt, and he can't drive out of there—If anything happens to him——' Her voice rose hysterically.

To her dismay, Vienna found herself saying briskly, 'I'd better go with him, then, I suppose.'

She didn't sound very gracious. She didn't feel very gracious. She felt resentful, even a little fearful, although the journey didn't really threaten to be hazardous.

But it wasn't going to do her any good staying around the homestead, watching Myra fret. From the look of her Myra was going to spend the time consumed with anxiety for her feckless son, growing more distraught every minute.

Vienna hurried to her room and changed into jeans and a shirt with long sleeves. She added her only pair of walking shoes, stout duty shoes from the hospital, and collected the wide-brimmed hat.

Neil drove the Range Rover to the steps and loaded up. He wasn't limping at all, and brushed aside his mother's anxieties with impatience; but Vienna detected a flicker of relief crossing his expression when he saw that she was coming with him, an added jauntiness, although he made no comment.

Vienna filled extra flasks with water, because the sky was clear and the sun looked like coming down hot and strong.

Myra in an untypical gesture clasped her arm

with her nervous fingers. Her eyes filled with apologetic tears.

'Be careful, dear, won't you? Don't let him go too far or travel anywhere dangerous.'

To Myra, all deserts were inhabited with a thousand threats. She shook her head dismally while Neil pointed out the Range Rover's strong bodywork, and reminded her that they probably wouldn't encounter a single danger on the whole journey.

'It's the fringe we're going to, Mother,' he elaborated. 'We won't really go into it. And we'll be back before three o'clock. You can start worrying after that if we don't arrive—that's a promise! We'll be back for late lunch, so don't worry.'

Myra wasn't convinced. She whispered, 'Do take good care. You really will, won't you?' and her eyes were haunted, so that Vienna knew she was really saying, 'Thank you for going with him, because I don't want anything to happen to either of you.'

She clung to Vienna's arm until Neil called irritably, 'Hurry up! I just told you, we've got to get back before the others.'

And Vienna thought, Yes, we do. We most certainly do. It would be difficult enough facing those critical eyes when Bren returned and discovered they had been using his vehicle on a wild goose chase in the desert. But at the thought of driving back and finding him waiting wrathfully after he'd spent his valuable time fixing their car, she found herself recoiling ... Never. No, never ...

They *must* reach Glenister before Bren and Terry. That way, at least they could choose their moment of confession. Not that Neil would look

on it as a confession, he had no qualms about what
he was doing, but Vienna had qualms enough for
both of them.

Neil was excited. He whistled and sang as they
drove out the homestead gateway and across the
dusty paddocks. He would have liked Vienna to
sing with him, little snatches of pop songs and old
ballads. He nodded and smiled at her, and pointed
to his throat, but Vienna couldn't share his confidence.

She remembered Myra pleading, 'Take care of
yourself,' and the next step of course was to recall
the big man's face, sharp-planed in the shadows
last night, as he leaned down and repeated
Dorothy's warning. Walk with your eyes wide
open.

Why couldn't she shake away her tremors and
share Neil's pleasure in the hot, hazy morning?

Dust flew up behind them as they drove, and
once they startled a gathering of banded parrots
beside a waterhole. The birds flew about in an ex-
plosion of green and yellow. Later a flock of corellas scattered from the branches of a tree, fluttering
like pieces of wild white paper in the blue sky, their
yellow underwings gleaming.

It should have been wonderful. Even when they
left Glenister's boundary and entered the wild red-
orange of the desert, it could still have been enchanting. Vienna saw a pair of emus running, long-
legged and dignified, through spinifex and spindly
scrub. She watched them until they blended into
the landscape and disappeared.

The Aboriginals had pointed out the humpbacked mountain for Neil to use as a landmark; but
as the desert flattened out it seemed the distance
between them and the rocky outcropping stretched

as they travelled. They drove for twenty miles, and the humpbacked mountain seemed no nearer. They covered another twenty, still it hovered on the horizon like a deceitful mirage.

There were other outcroppings of rocks, east-west running eruptions that scarred the land like dry bones. There were a few wild figs, occasional lonely groups of desert oaks, and enormous ghost gums with trunks and branches gleaming white. And of course the spinifex, clumps of it thrusting needle-points to harass and repel intruders.

Heat haze increased so that trees swam in the distance like seaweed under water. The ground became harsher, less sand, more rocks. Sometimes a stretch of loose stony ground set the steering-wheel spinning in Neil's hand. Several times they struggled over rises with stones plummeting down-hill behind them, the four-wheel-drive lurching while Neil fought grimly for control.

Vienna watched with anxiety, trying not to worry too much about the snail-trails of perspiration trickling from his forehead to his jaw; the jaw she had once thought so strong and reliable, and now found herself assessing as stubborn and childishly determined . . .

Despite the wrenched ankle, Neil handled the vehicle well. He was certainly tenacious. Another man might have given up and settled for a drive across the spinifex, or a visit to one of the rocky gorges, but Neil set his mind grimly on the hump-backed mountain.

Heat seeped into the cabin and Vienna found her hair sticky against her cheeks. Apart from that it was bearable, even with the bounce and clatter of broken sticks and flying stones.

And then at last, just when she thought it impossible, they reached their destination. The humpbacked mountain sat on the desert like a stone monster from pre-history, hunched over and dreaming. The arched back was bare rock, the lower part of its body hidden by foothills. The ascent was appallingly steep.

Neil wanted to set the Range Rover at it right away, but Vienna begged for a rest.

'I'm thirsty, Neil. Can't we have a break, and eat our sandwiches?'

He said sharply, 'Aren't you in a hurry, then? Don't you want to get back before they do?'

He didn't say Bren's name or Terry's either; and Vienna realised that he was feeling put-down because of his mistake with the horse, and pranging the car; and she thought, Oh God, why do they always say catastrophes happen in threes? Surely nothing can go wrong today.

Years of nursing had taught her to show plenty of confidence when she might be feeling alarm. She produced it now. She smiled at Neil and said, 'We'll travel better if we have a cup of tea, don't you think? Anyway, there's a small waterhole, and we mightn't see another. I'd like to cool my face.'

It worked. Neil switched off the motor and admitted, 'I guess you're right, Nurse. You usually are.'

Neil had never called her Nurse before. The word brought another sharp reminder of Brenden Darcour, one that she could have done without; but she shrugged it away. Bren was busy fixing Neil's car.

And before they left tomorrow, as they were certain to do, she would tell him finally, even put it in writing if he wanted, that she did not desire Evelyn Harryn's share of Red Vistas, and for what it was worth, he could have it.

For what it was worth ... The phrase gave her an uneasy lurch in the stomach. Practically nothing at all, that was how much it was worth.

So what did you offer a man after you'd used and abused his hospitality, and inconvenienced him by behaving in an utterly shabby way and totally without concern for him?

When you could see it all in his clear, cold, contemptuous eyes: that you rated for nothing, either, and were entirely worth forgetting, and that was exactly what he intended doing as soon as you were out of his sight.

Vienna poured cold drinks for herself and Neil after the tea and sandwiches, and asked with determined brightness, 'Must you have those rocks? I'd really much rather stay here.'

He stared at her in disbelief.

'Stay here? It's a pretty desolate place for a picnic, isn't it? What do you want to do—sit around and fry in the sun?'

'No.' That was quite true, anyway. The few scraggy trees offered only sparse shade. Neil had parked the Range Rover close to the only sizeable tree in sight, an ancient ghost gum. A sloping overhang jutted at one end of the shallow water-hole and they sat beneath it, drinking. There were no birds here; they had all taken shelter from the heat. But there were flies and insects, and the wind scooped up sand in flying wisps, so that plumes of orange and red dust rose and fell like mist on a river.

The wind had ever-increasing heat in it, and Neil muttered, 'Come on, let's get going.'

But his smile was the boyish gleam that he had been reserving for Luci since their arrival at

Glenister. He said, 'I say, Vee, it was pretty decent of you to come. I know you didn't want to.'

She dropped a pebble into the brown water and watched it sink and said lightly, 'Don't give it a thought.' Then she found his keen glance searching her face, as if he really cared about her reaction.

She said frankly, 'Your mother was worried. Nearly frantic.'

'Oh.' His look was crestfallen. 'I thought you might have cared about me.'

She had hurt his pride, what there was left of it, and she made an attempt at apology.

'Of course I cared about you. You're apt to be impulsive, you know. You must place great store on those bits of rock you're after, to take all this risk.'

'What risk?' He was genuinely surprised.

'Your ankle. It can't have been easy, driving over this rough country. And—and travelling where there aren't roads. And you could get sunstroke.'

Neil laughed and flung an arm carelessly around her shoulders.

'You do care,' he decided, and she let him think so, because this was not the time for soul-searching or discussion of what they might be feeling for each other. This was the time, she knew with cold certainty, when she must be taking care. The time to walk with her eyes wide open.

They were gathering up what remained of the sandwiches and tea when the camels appeared, a bull with his two females, stalking majestically from the lowest foothill along the flatter ground towards the Range Rover. The bull came first—he stayed with head erect, haughtily inspecting the vehicle, the females shifting curiously behind him, spreading out to view the Range Rover more clearly.

So curious they were, circling about and scenting the air, ruminating on the strange object that had suddenly appeared on their territory. Vienna wondered uneasily whether they had come to the waterhole to drink, and how they would regard the presence of two strangers, but after a few minutes the bull gave a low bellow, and the group stalked on. They moved without haste; the desert was theirs.

When the camels had passed, Neil and Vienna took the remnants of their picnic snack back to the Range Rover; but when Neil started up the motor and charged defiantly at the harsh slope of the first foothill, the engine coughed, spluttered, and was silent. Frowning, he let the vehicle roll back to level ground. His face clouded as he glanced down at the fuel gauge.

'Lord,' he said, 'we're empty. I didn't expect to use juice as fast as that.' And looking at Vee's concerned face, 'Don't panic, love. We've got plenty to get us back—I told you, I came prepared. I'll fill up before we climb the mountain, then all we have to do is hop in and take off when we get back. So don't worry.'

Shaking his head, astonished by her apprehension, he collected jerry-can and funnel, filled the tank, checked the gauge. Then he collected his binoculars and grinned at her cheerfully before he turned his face towards the mountain.

'Leg-power, I'm afraid. We'd better not waste petrol. Now for the top, and the diggings on the other side.'

He still believed he could do it. He carried the binoculars with the strap around his neck, as if

they were some kind of talisman that would show
him the way to his treasure-trove. Even when they
found themselves faced with a jagged split halfway
up the first foothill, it didn't deter him. He collected
a dead treetrunk and flung it over to make a bridge.
It was as if he were on a high, soaring with excitement, determined to get what he had come for.

Vienna followed him slowly, watching to see
whether he limped, because then she would be
entitled to demand a halt. She jammed the wide-
brimmed hat down over her forehead and trudged
behind him. Occasionally she looked up, and after
they had stumbled what seemed like miles, she
found a small dark cloud, sulphur-edged, hanging
over the mountaintop like a tattered flag.

Not without foreboding, she watched its ink-
smudge against the sky. One cloud didn't make a
storm, but she looked back wistfully at the Range
Rover . . . back and down. It seemed quite a way.
And as she gazed below her, one of the camels
bolted suddenly from behind a foothill. This time
he was not curious. Head thrust forward, yellow
froth bubbling on open lips, he passed the Range
Rover as if it were not there. Something had
frightened him.

Vienna watched him go, with sinking heart. The
omens were changing . . .

Neil's shout from well above her called her back
to the mountain.

'Come on! You'll never get anywhere mooning
around!'

Wordlessly after that they climbed. The only
sounds were the scuffle of loose stones underfoot,
wind echoing in the weird rock formations, and
their own laboured breathing.

Vienna decided several times they would never

reach the top, and when they did she lay out-
stretched on a warm slab of rock, because there
were no cool sheltered places. She hated to think
how hot those rocks might have been had not the
wind driven a veil of cloud between them and the
bare heat of the sun. The thought startled her. A
veil of cloud——

She jerked upright, staring at the sky. There were
cloud-banks overhead now, rolling like smoke from
a ship's funnel. Dark moving shapes edged with
swirls of sulphur-yellow.

Neil wasn't concerned. He scanned the ground
on the far side of the humpbacked mountain
through the binoculars, while Vienna watched the
wind play tricks with patches of sand. Pieces of
dry spinifex grass skittered across the ground where
the Range Rover sat like a child's toy in the orange
desert. Once there was a rumbling sound. It could
have come from mountain or clouds. It didn't dis-
tract Neil. He stood determinedly scanning the
land on the far side of the mountain, finding
nothing that looked like the scars of old diggings.

Vienna didn't care about the honey opal and the
coloured quartz. She regretted Neil's disappointment, but as clouds piled up so did her misgivings.

Neil held the binoculars out to see.

'Want to see?'

'I can see it.'

'With the glasses, I mean.'

She took the binoculars. 'It's very—very vast—
and beautiful,' she said warily. 'But there aren't
any diggings, and it's getting late.'

'Wait a minute.'

He took the glasses and resumed searching, as if
he couldn't accept that he hadn't found what he
was looking for. The diggings must be down there

somewhere, but it was too late now to go and look.

Another roll of thunder sounded and Neil looked warily at the sky. He hated leaving without getting what he had come for.

'We'll have to go,' he admitted. 'It's getting late.' Too late, Vienna thought, watching the clouds roll, measuring with her fear the distance they had to scramble back to the Range Rover.

A few heavy drops fell. Not really rain, just a reminder that there were showers up there, waiting ... Neil was fitting the binoculars resentfully back into their case when the lightning struck. Neither of them saw it coming, but they heard it. And the thunder. Vienna had always known lightning as a silent white flash in the sky. Now it came down hissing and crackling as it hit the top of the hump-backed mountain. It was very close. Not near enough to harm them; but she felt her body flinch as it struck. Her mind too numb to think, she waited for the next flash. Neil grabbed her hand and half-wrestled her as he dragged her down the slope and into the shelter of a split in the rock. His tender ankle must have taken punishment as they stumbled over loose rocks.

They huddled there while the storm broke, Vienna shivering because the lightning had found her on the mountaintop when she should have been safe from storms. They crouched in the cleft until the electrical storm rolled over, and she saw gratefully that Neil was sheltering her with his body. Once he turned to look at her, his expression guilty.

'You were right, lady—I should never have dragged you out here.'

'I'm glad you did.'

'You're glad!' He didn't believe her, but it was true. Tomorrow, next week, maybe even as long as she lived, she would remember the fear and the escape. She would say, 'Nothing is ever quite as terrible as you fear it's going to be'—and with a bit of luck she might believe it. All through the empty years . . .

When the storm quietened, they scrambled back to the ground. Neil gave her a cheeky grin as he opened the door of the Range Rover.

'I'm glad you appreciated the experience.' He was grateful she had decided to make the best of it. He turned the key in the ignition, and the motor responded, sputtered and died. He stared at the fuel gauge incredulously. It showed Empty.

'Oh, lord! Our fuel-tank's been milked—it must have been.'

But when they got out and walked carefully around the vehicle a smell of petrol hung in the air.

Neil muttered finally, 'Fuel leak.' He sounded defeated, as if he had suffered enough sabotage for one short holiday. He ran his fingers through his hair, leaving dirt-streaks across his forehead, down his cheeks. He leaned against the side of the Range Rover and slapped his thighs with his hands, beating out his frustration.

'This country,' he groaned. 'This rotten, rotten country!'

Something on that jolting journey, pointed mulga stake or sharp-edged rock, had holed the petrol tank. Neil didn't waste time searching for the damage. He had no more fuel, anyway. He stumbled to the ancient ghost gum and sat down once again leaning his face on his hands.

Vienna poured two mugs of water. She said

calmly, 'We'll just have to wait, won't we?'

Myra knew where they had gone. Neil had been
voluble, explaining about the humpbacked mountain to allay his mother's fears. So when Bren and
Terry got back from Red Vistas they would know
where to come searching. Bren would come . . .

Vienna told herself dismally, 'If he doesn't decide
to leave us here overnight, which would serve us
right,' but she didn't believe he would do that. No
matter how tired he was, or how disgusted, he
would point the utility in the direction of the desert
and its phantom diggings, and move on. But how
angry he would be! His Range Rover and two of
his guests had whisked themselves out to the desert
and hadn't made it back.

How long would he wait before deciding they
must be lost or disabled? If he had to travel in the
dark—Vienna shivered. She walked to the waterhole and splashed her face and hands. It didn't relieve her anxiety, but at least she felt cooler. She
combed her hair and shook dust out of her clothing, then she rinsed out the empty jerry-can and
filled it with water and took it to Neil.

'Pour it over your hands and feet,' she ordered
calmly. 'Don't drink it, there might be petrol
fumes.'

Neil cheered up when she unwound the bandage
and found the ankle not much the worse for wear.
He said, surprised, 'Well, that's one trick we've
taken,' and allowed himself a faint grin.

Once he said, 'I wonder when they'll come,' and
again later, 'Maybe they won't find us until tomorrow, if they were held up at Red Vistas.'

Vienna wasn't afraid of staying in the desert all
night, but she didn't really fancy it. What she
fancied was getting back to Glenister Two as

quickly as possible and facing the lash of Bren's tongue and having it over and done with, crawling away into some dark corner to hide her embarrassment. They had bungled this whole thing dreadfully, and would come out of it as they deserved . . . pride in shreds. The man with the distant eyes would put as much distance between them as he possibly could after today's adventure, and she wouldn't blame him. Not even if he left them out all night with the dingoes and whatever other creatures inhabited the sand, rock and stones.

Meanwhile, they ought to look for the nearest shelter. Neil scrambled to his feet saying, 'The clouds are breaking up,' and Vienna didn't know whether that would turn out to be a good or bad thing; but when sun straggled through broken cloud she was pleased, because the air cleared, so they would see the utility sooner as it approached . . . *if* it approached . . .

Her head drummed because of the humidity. Neil fussed about making them comfortable under the ledge of rock where they had eaten their sandwiches earlier. He was being humble. 'I'm an idiot,' he confessed. 'You should be screeching at me.'

Vienna sighed. 'I don't suppose it's idiotic to want to see everything you can while you're here. We were just unlucky.'

He gave her a surprised look, and the boyishness came back into his smiling.

'It's rather splendid of you to see it that way.' Ruefully, he examined her hot cheeks, the damp hair clinging to her forehead. 'It eases my conscience. You're a darn good sport, Vee. Thank goodness you're with me—I'd hate to be stranded out here on my own.'

He coaxed her pleasantly into the shade. 'Siesta

time,' he announced.

The last thing Vienna recorded before dozing off in the heat was a sharp edge of rock pushing into her spine, finding a tender place that reminded her of the other time when she had been bruised and scratched and a tall quiet man had cradled her in his arms and blended his strength with hers.

She murmured drowsily, 'Dorothy Green saw lightning in my tea-cup. Wasn't that weird?'

'Not really.' Neil wasn't given to wild imaginings. 'You can concoct anything you like out of tea-leaves. She ought to use a tea-strainer.'

'Terry said that.' Her head was floating as she settled back into her patch of shade.

But it hadn't been 'anything' that Dorothy saw among the tea-leaves. It had been lightning; and the lightning had hissed and crackled, had struck and gone, leaving her shaken but unharmed. Yet she would never feel the same about an electrical storm again. Every lightning-streak would come complete with sound, and sometimes she would imagine herself back on the mountaintop . . .

Or had the tea-leaves foretold the other kind of lightning—the blinding flash of comprehension when you looked at a man and made the earth-shattering discovery that *this* man, and only this man, could change the whole colour of your life, if he wanted. Could hold your heart in his strong hands, set your responses on fire with his strong body, tease your imagination with his strong mind . . . Because you loved him . . . only him . . .

'Quiet!' Vienna ordered herself, and settled back to drowse.

It didn't seem much later that a pair of birds disturbed her as they competed for water and tree space; but the sun had moved across the sky and the rock-hollows were turning purple. The old tree beside the Range Rover cast a long shadow, and the humpbacked mountain wore a golden stripe along its back; while in the east a plume of dust rose and fanned out and vanished, only to reappear closer. They were being rescued.

Neil stirred, and Vienna aroused him by shaking his shoulder. He must have seen from her expression that it was important, because he was instantly alert, standing up in a swift movement. He steadied himself, holding on to a dry tree-root wedged between rocks, and after he had looked at the westering sun he turned and searched the other way, and saw the approaching plume of dust.

He made a try at jauntiness.

'Here comes teacher—wonder if he's brought his cane.'

But he straightened his shoulders, and Vienna knew that whatever happened next Neil had done some growing up during the long, hot afternoon.

So Myra had something to be grateful for, although perhaps if she had allowed her son to grow up sooner, he might not have been stranded here, waiting to be told what an outsize idiot he was.

Vienna wondered whether they ought to do some kind of signalling, but Neil thought not.

'They can see the Range Rover,' he added gruffly; and sure enough the utility headed straight for it.

Vienna and Neil walked to the four-wheel-drive and stood beside it until the utility drew up. The ute wore a heavy plastering of dust, so they had not stopped to clean it down after the trip to Red Vistas. Vienna imagined how the two men must have felt when they discovered themselves faced with another journey into heat and rough country.

Both Bren and Terry alighted stiffly. Their dust-streaked faces were weary, but Terry spoke cheerfully. His smile made Vienna want to weep with gratitude.

'You're both all right, then?'

They had brought with them a young Aboriginal, one of the stockmen Vienna had already met. His name was Johnno, he had brown velvet eyes like Noreen and Jenny, and a fine intelligent face; and he, too, was smiling. But there was no smile on the face of the boss-man. If he had brought Johnno with him, probably he had expected they might be lost and he would have some tracking to do.

The stern eyes flickered over Vienna in remote but penetrating assessment, before they inspected Neil and the vehicle. His voice was terse.

'What happened?'

Neil licked dry lips. 'Sorry, old chap—can't tell you how sorry. I'm afraid we've sprung a fuel leak. I carried spare patrol, but we've done the lot.'

Terry nodded. 'Occupational hazard.' He grinned. 'Fix it in a jiffy if it's only a hole in the tank. Easy enough to patch it up enough to drive back—we've got spare petrol.'

'I can drive——' Neil's voice was tentative, and nobody listened.

Terry lay on his back and disappeared under the vehicle, while Johnno squatted beside him. Occasionally they talked in low voices. When Terry squirmed from under the vehicle he gave Bren a nod.

'Can do,' he announced. 'Johnny and I can handle it, if you want to drive the others home.'

But Bren shook his head. 'We'll wait. Do you want a hand?'

'Nope. Too many cooks and all that.'

Vienna saw with fascination that Terry worked his eyebrows while he talked, just as Jo-Jo did. 'We'll put on a temporary patch. It'll last till we get home. Won't take long.'

Vienna hunched alongside the tree while Terry and Johnno plugged the fuel leak. The big man came and settled beside her. He brought her a cold drink, and she wrinkled her nose at its taste.

'Salt!' she exclaimed.

'Just what you need.'

He was hot and weary, shirt wet with perspiration. The tips of his eyelashes were dust-speckled, and the lines on his face had deepened into grooves. Perspiration and dust and the energy-aura he carried with him combined into a powerful mansmell. It was not unpleasant. His hard strong hands were caked with red and orange dust-streaks, and he grimaced as she handed him the empty glass.

'You didn't pick up any treasure, Sister Maddern?'

His voice was mocking, but Vienna didn't feel like entering a slanging match. She felt guilty and desperately tired, because it seemed that every move they made brought more disaster.

She said, 'Will it be hard to fix, the leak?' and he shook his head.

'No. You can do it with chewing-gum if you happen to have any. Or glue, even soap.' When she looked surprised he added slyly, 'Soap is very useful in its place.' He was thinking of the water-hole, she knew.

Bren pushed the black Stetson on to the back of his head, and she looked at him covertly and saw his forehead damp with sweat, the blond hair darkened and limp and tousled.

He must have sensed her distress, for he moved closer, his arm brushing her shoulder as he rummaged in his shirt pocket for a cigarette.

'Relax,' he ordered roughly. 'If I murder anybody over this little escapade it won't be you.'

She said in a small voice that didn't sound like her own, 'I suppose everybody is worried. Myra——'

'Jumping out of her skin with the horrors. Beset by visions of her son's bleached bones lying out in the desert——'

'N-not very funny.'

'No, it wasn't.' His mouth was stern. 'Still under the maternal wing, isn't he, your boy-friend?'

'He considers his mother's feelings, yes. You may c-consider that a weakness.'

If her voice was going to shake like that she'd better not carry this conversation any farther. She hadn't been afraid to stay in the desert overnight. Rescue had arrived before fear had time to push its way deeply into her imagination. It was the boss of Glenister Two who shook her, sitting there with his sand-streaked face and his lips compressed, jawbone pushing against the taut tanned skin as if private emotions were being kept under control there.

Of course he was angry. Of course his patience had run out. And he must be wondering wrathfully whatever else they could possibly do to him before they finally went on their way, out of his life for ever. That'll be something for him to celebrate, she told herself dismally.

He said abruptly, 'Well, at least you had enough sense to stay on the ground. You didn't do anything outrageously stupid like trying to climb the mountain.'

Dear God! Just when she'd decided the worst of it was over; just as she had decided, well, now she had plunged the depths and it couldn't get any worse could it, and she'd survived hadn't she, even if morale was non-existent, just when . . .

Her lips parted slightly as if she might have spoken, but her complete vocabulary suddenly deserted her. There wasn't a word she could find to say to answer him. Not one word. She stared helplessly at her knees, then down to her dusty shoes and the cuffs of her jeans that looked as if she'd tramped a hundred miles. She swallowed unhappily, and even the swallowing was difficult.

Her miserable silence must have spoken for her, for he drew in a long, slow breath and when he let it out in a gusty sigh, she hunched her shoulders and kept staring steadfastly at her shoes, so that Bren wouldn't have a clue as to how devastated and utterly miserable she was.

She sat beside him with her composure falling in little pieces all around her. Once she had thought she needed a shoulder to weep on, and Neil hadn't been there. And she'd managed that time, hadn't she? So here it was again, another call for courage. She made a tremendous effort, straightened her shoulders and pulled her attention away from those pathetic dusty shoes that hadn't walked anywhere special, really, except into a mountain of trouble. Back to the flinty eyes of the man from Glenister who was looking at her as though completely dumbfounded by her stupidity.

Vienna said wretchedly, 'We didn't go out of sight—of your four-wheel-drive, I mean. W-we could look down and see it all the time.'

Her voice trailed away.

'People,' he answered harshly, 'have been known to die from heat exhaustion. You wouldn't have been the first.'

'I—I'm sorry we've been such a nuisance. I wish we hadn't.' As an apology, it was quite inadequate. Of course it was. They had been far, far more than a nuisance. They had repaid his help by throwing his routine into confusion, upsetting visitors, taking overseer and stockman from their duties. Wasting time, wasting fuel, damaging his vehicle——

'Forget it,' he ordered harshly. 'You can stop feeling sorry for yourself.' His voice was grittier than the desert sand.

It didn't take Terry and Johnno long to plug the hole in the petrol tank. They refuelled the Range Rover, started it up and turned towards home, signalling that all was well.

Bren looked over his shoulder at the hump-backed mountain as they stood up.

'We saw the lightning,' he said. 'How close was it?' He ignored Neil, who had come to stand close by. His question was for Vienna.

'Oh, it—it made a fizzing noise.'

'That close, was it?'

'Frightened the hell out of us,' Neil admitted cheerfully, but Bren had no answering smile for him.

Neil travelled back in the utility with Bren and Vienna. He wasn't very pleased about that, probably because it made him look somehow inadequate. He would have liked to drive the Range Rover up to the homestead in a show of bravado, but he made no protest when he was bundled aside, and Terry and Johnno took over.

The sunset crimsoned and disappeared before

they reached Glenister. Dorothy Green waited on the verandah, with Myra and Luci and Abby, and Vienna saw that although her greeting was cheerful her eyes were dark with worry. She had left a casserole in the Glenister oven, and they all sat down, after showers and change of clothing, to a late evening meal that was eaten in almost total silence.

Afterwards Abby, anxious to please, carried coffee into the sitting room, and everybody followed; but the uneasiness went with them. Abby steered Vienna to a comfortable chair and sat down on the wide arm, as close to Vienna as she could. She wore the unsuitable embroidered dress again, her face sharp and pale and older than her years. She reached down and squeezed Vienna's fingers, curling her hand around hers. When Bren walked across the room and stood over them both, Abby didn't move.

'Abby,' his voice was deep and powerful, 'how about putting on some music? I want to talk to Miss Maddern.'

Abby became suddenly animated.

'Uncle Bren, you promised to look at my drawings. You have to choose the ones you want for your cards. Remember?'

His voice crisped. 'They can wait, Abby. I'll see them tomorrow.'

Pink-cheeked, Abby faced him. Her fingers tightened around Vienna's, but she refused to move.

'*Now*, please, Uncle Bren. You promised! Come and look at them now.'

The tall man's jaw tightened as he stared down at his defiant niece, then miraculously his expression softened. He sighed resignedly, and surrendered.

'All right, Abby, I'll see them now.'

As Abby went for her sketchbook, he offered Vienna a crooked smile. He bent low, so that only she could hear his voice.

'St Georgette,' he whispered softly, 'has just rescued you from the dragon.'

If she hadn't been so weary, Vienna might have handled the situation better, but her face was hot and stiff with sunburn, her head drummed. Tears filled her eyes as Bren stood looking down at her. He made a small sound like a catching of breath, before he reached down and touched her hand, fingers curling over hers much as Abby's had done. Then Abby came and led him away, and he went quietly, without so much as a backward glance.

When she finished her coffee, Vienna mustered the last remnants of her dignity and as casually as she could—because Myra was looking at her with curiosity and Luci with hatred—she walked out of the room and on to the verandah, where she stood taking great gulps of cool night air. She breathed in the sweet mixed scents of the garden, and after a while somebody inside put on a record, and music drifted out to mingle with the fragrant night. Vienna bit her lip, because it was a song of un-requited love, and that was something she could have done without just now.

A little later the hum of voices became louder as a door opened and shut, and Vienna tensed as footsteps sounded behind her, but it wasn't Neil. Only the boss of Glenister Two could make her so aware of his presence that she did not need to turn her head and look at him to know that he was there. He stood behind her, so close she felt the warmth from his body. His hands curved over her shoulders, his voice whimsical and very soft.

'That must be an emotional sort of hospital you

work for, Sister Maddern, if they encourage you to burst into tears when the going gets rough.'

She protested fiercely, 'I do not burst into tears——' but was careful to keep her head averted so that he would not see her brimming eyes.

He took one hand away from her shoulder and lifted it, and she thought he intended touching her wet cheeks. Her whole body stiffened, shrinking from the humiliation. Instead, he gathered her swinging black hair in his palm and twisted it gently into a swathe, holding it so that the back of his hand lay against the nape of her neck in spine-tingling contact.

It was several seconds before she discovered she was holding her breath; and then she let it out, very slowly, very carefully, so that he would not guess the effect he was having on her. He took his left hand from her other shoulder and slid his arm over her breast and slowly down until it encircled her waist, then he pressed her slim body backwards until it leaned against him, so that she felt the warmth and strength and length of him comforting her, and once again her skin tingled at his touch. Was it her body that trembled, or was it his?

He said suddenly, 'Why didn't you tell me, Sister Maddern? I would have listened.'

'Tell you what?'

'That you didn't want to go on this wild jaunt this morning, but you let yourself be persuaded into it by Myra's motherly alarms?'

'If you know, then I don't need to tell you.' But she was relieved that he understood. Myra must have done that much for her, and she was grateful. It was foolish to care whether he blamed her, but the warmth of his body against hers was comforting, and she let herself relax.

Then somebody called her name, and Bren stiffened, his hands suddenly still.

'Your guardian angel is on my trail.' His voice was wry. 'A little over-protective, isn't she?'

Abby came out through a rectangle of light thrown by the open doorway behind her. Her footsteps echoed on the wood.

'Vienna—oh!' She studied them both doubtfully, and Vienna turning her head saw that Bren was smiling.

He let her go and stepped away from her, not in a hurried way but with deliberation, opening his hands for Abby's inspection.

'No stockwhip!' he mocked, before he turned and strode away, leaving them there, looking at each other with uncertainty.

Abby asked, her voice a whisper, 'Was he mad at you, Vee?'

'I suppose he was.' Vienna steered her indoors gently. 'He really is entitled to be angry, Abby.'

Abby nodded. 'But not with you,' she insisted loyally.

Vienna hoped the tear-stains on her cheeks weren't showing. As they re-entered the sitting room, Luci's shrewd eyes weren't missing any detail of her appearance. No doubt she'd noticed Bren follow her out on to the verandah. Well, Vee told herself hopefully, she wasn't looking too ruffled. Luci needn't read much into that little interlude out there among the night shadows and the glittering stars.

Her chair was still unoccupied, but Vienna didn't sit in it. She hoped Abby didn't mind, but reaction was setting in. She wanted to get to bed as quickly as possible. She said nervously, 'If nobody objects, I think I'll take myself off. I'm a little short on sleep.'

'We'll all go.' Neil had refused to allow Vienna
to dress his ankle. He had bandaged it himself,
remarking that neither climbing nor driving had
done it any harm. Now he stood without hesita-
tion, and when Myra looked as if she might have
fussed over him a little, he waved her away.

'If we're leaving tomorrow, we need all the sleep
we can get.'

'Are we going home tomorrow?' she asked.

'In the afternoon.' Neil looked surprised that
Vienna didn't know. 'First thing after lunch—that
leaves us all morning to rest. We're calling for an
evening meal and sleeping overnight at Kenora
station—special invitation. Bren arranged it.' His
grin was apologetic. 'If you're surprised anyone
would invite us, so am I. But there you are. Terry
says my car's set for the trip, so there's nothing to
keep us here.' When Myra made a small protesting
sound her added sternly, 'My ankle's all right,
Mother. It was only a minor twist, not even a
sprain. I was lucky.' Abby stared at Vienna with
mournful eyes. 'You can't go,' she pleaded, and
Vee said softly, 'I'll leave you my address in
Adelaide. We'll see each other.'

Luci shot her a look of undisguised hostility.
'Abby will be very busy. She has to catch up on all
the lessons she missed this week, through her own
naughtiness. She has a lot of work to do.'

Abby turned on Luci fiercely. 'I'm not going to
be all that busy. I'll see Vienna whenever I want
to!'

Her shrill passionate voice challenged, and Luci
snapped, 'Oh, you don't have to carry on about it.
Do what you like. Don't blame me if you can't
pass your exams!' Her eyes burned with antagonism

and her lush bright mouth curled with hostility.

'We'll have to pack.' Myra looked around her helplessly.

'Tomorrow.' Neil opened the door for her. His voice was edgy. 'Mother, we're all tired tonight. If we don't sleep we shan't get away at all.'

Abby hadn't expected them to leave so soon. Her stricken face was the last thing Vienna saw as she left the room and walked wearily along the passage. Inside her bedroom, she sat on the edge of the bed, being careful not to look in the bedside mirror, because she had the hollow conviction that her expression might resemble Abby's.

Of course it was only right they should leave as soon as they could. They had caused enough trouble.

Tiredly, she pulled her small suitcase from the wardrobe, because in the morning she must help Noreen and Jenny tidy out the rooms, so that they did not leave extra work for Dorothy when they left. But when it came to collecting her few clothes, she found herself too weary. So she allowed herself this one final luxury: that tomorrow she would pack, but tonight she would crawl into bed pretending everything was going on as it had been—that early in the morning she would get up, and cook breakfast, then she and Abby might find some twisted tree to sketch, or maybe another tawny frogmouth might sit and study them through slit eyes while they worked.

But she didn't really convince herself. Reality kept intruding.

The dream of Evelyn Harryn had brought her a long, long way from home. Now she must go back to where she belonged.

She would, she decided, put the painting of Red

Vistas away for a while. With luck, the day might come when she could hang it on the wall without wanting to shed tears over it. But not yet. Because Evelyn's dream belonged out here, among the red and orange earth and the cattle in the mulga; not in her little flat with its blue upholstery and harlequin cushions.

CHAPTER EIGHT

NEXT morning for the first time since their arrival Vienna failed to wake for early breakfast.

A subdued Abby knocked on her door with a tray of steak and eggs and toast, and when Vienna blinked at her in sleepy astonishment, she said miserably, 'Thought I might as well do something useful. Uncle Bren said not to wake you earlier.'

'Oh dear, I wish you had. I'm quite capable, Abby. I'm not heatstruck or anything dramatic, just sleepy.'

A faint grin lifted Abby's gloom.

'Luci's getting everyone else's breakfast. She's not a bit pleased, but Uncle Bren said she had to. He reckoned Terry'd be a bit tired this morning, so he wouldn't let Luci disturb Dorothy.'

'Oh, darn! Why ever didn't you wake me, Abby? Now I feel guilty.'

'It's all right.' Abby shrugged her thin shoulders. She sat on Vienna's bed and watched gloomily while she ate her steak and eggs.

'Luci's furious. It's the first bit of work she's done this trip, and she reckons Dorothy had better come back and get meals now you're leaving.' She sighed mournfully. 'I wish you were staying longer, Vee. I wanted it so much last night I wished on just about every star in the sky. I wanted to finish my Christmas cards before I went home.'

'Can't you carry on with them in Adelaide? You've lots of time before Christmas.'

'I know.' Abby's mouth drooped. 'But it won't

be the same without you. I don't think I'll bother.'

'Abby, what kind of artist will you be, if you get defeated so easily?' queried Vienna sternly.

Abby's smile flickered.

'I'm sorry—I really am. And I'll try; but it's all going to be so different without you.'

She hovered miserably until Vee finished breakfast, then carried the tray back to the kitchen.

Vienna showered and dressed in the fawn slacks and a yellow cotton shirt and tied her hair back with a narrow yellow ribbon. Now was the time to pack her suitcase. Now, before she let herself sit around and brood about what she was doing, and how she would never see Bren again. Now, quickly, before she let herself realise that she was going back to Adelaide to discover the real meaning of the word 'lonely'.

She folded her blouses and skirts. She was packing the cream shoes with the broken heel when she realised she was not alone. Glenister's boss lounged in her open doorway, his face impassive.

'What the devil do you think you're doing?'

Vienna turned her back. That ought to show him she had no time for him this morning.

'I'm packing,' she retorted. 'That's obvious, isn't it? We're going home this afternoon, remember?'

A strange gentleness softened the stern mouth, easing away some of the frostiness from the cold eyes.

'Walking out on Abby, are you?'

She swung around then, goaded into reply.

'What else am I supposed to do—hitch-hike home?'

'Well,' he offered thoughtfully, 'you could do the right thing by the child, and help her over the next few days. The mail plane is due then. If you are determined to leave, you could fly back in the mail plane with Luci and Abby. I think that's what Abby needs from you, don't you?'

She looked at him in anguish.

'I came here with Neil. How can I stay, when he's leaving? His ankle——'

'Has healed remarkably quickly. I don't think it was much hurt in the first place. He got more a fright than anything when he was thrown.'

'So how can I stay?'

'Easily. Just put those things back in the wardrobe and get on with the job, there's a good girl.' His face creased in a flash of quiet amusement. 'Luci isn't very happy doing your chores. She'll have to slave over a hot stove if you leave. I won't allow Dorothy to be imposed on. Terry needs a rest.'

Yes, Terry needed a rest, Vienna was sure he did. And Abby needed security, the kind of security she might never have had, because she lacked parents. Because she was a strange little girl who had learned to live mostly within herself and not cry for help, except on that one occasion not long ago when she had run away.

She hesitated, and looked down at her half-packed case. Bren watched her quietly, face impassive.

'You owe Abby.' His face was stern.

'Neil won't like it.'

'He probably won't. But he'll survive. I've contacted Kenora Station and arranged for him and Myra to stay overnight there. If his ankle weakens, he'll be looked after until he's fit enough to tackle the rest of the journey.'

'Won't they mind?'

'No.' Almost as an afterthought he added, 'It's my property.'

She might have known. Of course it was. That was why he had spent so much time in the office with Melly Taeger on the way up.

He watched her carefully, leaning indolently against the doorway; but his eyes were intent, registering the emotions flitting over her expressive face.

She was to have another few days at Glenister Two. Foolish, probably, prolonging the pain. But beggars couldn't be choosers, and she was a beggar now . . . three more days of his company, no matter whether she only saw him passing, or at mealtimes.

He added softly, 'You might consider something else, too.'

'Such as?'

'Such as getting rid of that object you're still wearing on your finger.' He nodded towards the emerald ring. 'It doesn't belong there—I don't believe it ever did. If you were an honest young woman, you'd admit it. What's the matter? Can't you make a decision? Don't you have a mind of your own?'

'Of all the nerve——' Her eyes flashed, and he laughed and said,

'That's better. And for heaven's sake unpack that case and settle down. Do you want me to break the news to your ever-loving fiancé and his mother that you're not travelling just yet?'

'No, I'll tell him.'

'Don't forget Abby.' His voice deepened. 'It seems you've become very important to her. She ought to know you're staying.'

He did care about Abby, then. She saw concern in his sudden gravity. Of course he cared.

She said impulsively, 'You arranged it, so you tell Abby.' And then she added, 'I'll talk to Neil.'

Although she didn't mention the ring she saw him glance quickly down at her finger before he turned and walked away.

She had been prepared to find it difficult telling Neil, but she found him strangely agreeable. She offered him his ring and he said, 'Look here, Vee, we'll talk about this when we get home,' but he accepted the ring and put it carefully away in his wallet.

It wasn't very good for her ego, that he should accept it so willingly. Perhaps he had appreciated Luci's feminine wiles, her clinging hands, her wanton eyes.

He said awkwardly, 'Maybe we acted too quickly.' And she thought, *We* acted ... I don't recall having very much say in the arrangement ... then felt instantly remorseful, because that was pretty weak, claiming you'd been hustled into an engagement you'd wanted with all your heart at the time.

Neil must be feeling guilty, because he talked fast, with exaggerated cheerfulness. Between sentences he smiled at her, a little too brightly, using the ingratiating look that had once touched her heart. Vienna recognised it now for what it signified. That Neil was a young man taking a long time about growing up, and he hadn't quite got there yet.

She wanted him to stop talking. She said, 'I suppose our temperaments didn't match as well as we hoped,' and he agreed quickly—much too quickly.

'Yes. You do tend to carry on a bit, you know, without consulting a fellow. It's a habit some nurses get——' His voice trailed off.

'You mean——' Vienna kept her own voice level but anger was rising, 'you mean, I'm bossy.'

'I didn't say exactly that.' He studied her uneasily. 'All I'm saying is that you've a mind of your own. You're not—you're never going to be—a clinging vine, are you?'

'Of course I'm not,' she snapped.

'It's a manner some nursing Sisters get,' he elaborated, trying to explain without giving offence. 'A tone of voice, because they're so used to giving orders and seeing they're carried out. Mother pointed it out to me once. "You'll never get on well with one of your staff nurses in your private life," she told me, and I guess she was right. I mean, a man doesn't like to be continually told what to do. And you're not always very agreeable.'

A bubble of laughter exploded somewhere deep under the skin of Vienna's emotions and broke into a thousand glittering prisms of joy. So she was bossy, was she? The master of Glenister Two would be amused to hear that. Hadn't he just told her she was indecisive?

She said, 'Safe journey, Neil. I hope your ankle doesn't cause you any trouble,' and he looked as if he might have kissed her, and then decided against it.

He said awkwardly, 'When we get home——' and Vienna answered,

'Yes, when we get home——'

And that was all. Neither of them believed it.

Vienna walked slowly into the kitchen and arranged for Noreen and Jenny to come back later and tidy out the rooms when they were emptied. She stood in the kitchen, savouring the fact that she would be working there for a little while longer.

Abby appeared, clutching sketchbook and pencils. Bren had told her the news. Her eyes shone, but she handled her emotions extremely well, keeping her delight well under control as she casually poured herself a glass of orange juice, drank, rinsed the glass, and turned to walk away.

She said casually, 'Good thing you're staying, Vee. I'll be in the garden if you don't want me in here this morning.'

Vienna said no, everything in the homestead was fine.

Luci had disappeared. She had not been seen since Vienna entered the kitchen.

Abby added gruffly, 'Uncle Bren says if I want to do more than dabble I'd better get on with my sketching,' and Vienna nodded approval.

So Abby walked outside to follow the footsteps of Ralph Darcour, who had once painted a picture that brought ease to a dying woman he had never known.

Vienna went over the contents of fridge and freezer, then went to see what Myra would like for lunch before she and Neil left on the first leg of their journey. She saw immediately that Neil had been there before her. Myra was gracious but relieved. She had become fond of Vienna, but she still didn't consider a member of the nursing staff an ideal mate for her son.

Myra, too, must have been feeling guilty about yesterday. Her greeting to Vienna was warm, if guarded.

She commented affably, 'So we're not to have your company on the way home?' and Vienna said no, she was staying with Abby for another few days.

Myra pursed her lips doubtfully,

'Ah yes, the strange little girl.'

Myra considered Abby a mouselike and un-interesting child, and thought it extremely odd for a girl her age to be wandering about drawing things, instead of taking part in the usual activities of children her age. But she was prepared to grant her sympathy, because everything appeared to be working out very well. There was even in the back of her mind a faint hope that Neil might in Adelaide resume acquaintance with the girl, Luci, who seemed a much more suitable companion for her son.

Some of the bloom was missing from Myra's carefully tended complexion. Vienna saw with compassion that yesterday had proved as much an ordeal for her as it had been for her son. Worse, perhaps, for she had had to wait and worry.

Vienna explained gently, 'We weren't in any real trouble yesterday—at least, not so long as there was someone to come and get us. I hope you weren't too worried.'

'Naturally I was—I was—upset. Neil is so very like his father, so impetuous.' Myra had faced devils yesterday and she hadn't quite recovered. Her voice quavered. 'I don't know whether he told you, but Neil's father died on—on a mountain-climbing expedition. In New Zealand, it was. He shouldn't have gone, he was too inexperienced for that sort of excursion. But he wouldn't admit it. Of course that was a—a long time ago.'

She offered Vienna a taut smile that was only a movement of her lips. 'Everybody has their troubles,' she said. 'I shouldn't have burdened you with mine. And—and thank you for yesterday. I would have been even more concerned about my son if you hadn't been with him.'

Myra's packing was almost finished. Vienna straightened the last few garments and located a plastic bag to hold shoes.

'Would you like a drink?' she offered impulsively. 'Brandy, perhaps? Or a pot of tea on the verandah?'

'Tea on the verandah, thank you. You're very thoughtful, my dear.'

Myra might have been troubled by her lack of warmth towards the future daughter-in-law she had just lost. She touched Vienna's arm.

'If I ever have to go to one of those places some day—a nursing home, like Neil's hospital——' she gulped unhappily, 'I do hope there's somebody like you—to talk to.'

Now the packing was completed, and Vienna bent down to close and lock the lid, but Myra shook her head with its shining lavender-tinted hair, and waved her away.

'Neil will come,' she said simply.

Out on the verandah they sat at the little cane table, drinking tea. Vienna poured a cup for Bren and put biscuits on the saucer; and when she tapped on the office door and entered, he looked up, raising his eyebrows, thanking her without speaking. He worked on a column of figures in a book, and Vienna didn't stay.

Neil and Luci came back from a quick dip in the pool, and Abby's ears must have been tuned, because she followed a few minutes later.

Luci had seen Vienna emerge from the office. She snapped, 'You didn't take Bren tea mid-morning, did you? He won't drink it. He'll prefer something cold. I'd better go and see what he wants.'

She came out of the office, looking put out, and flounced petulantly to the table on the verandah. So Bren had decided to settle for a cup of tea this morning, and Vienna sipped her own tea quietly, being careful not to show she noticed.

It seemed to her that the homestead had a kind of quietness over it after Neil and his mother drove away that afternoon; a hush, as though some kind of crisis had come and gone. She went for a solitary swim, then dressed and wandered around the gardens, looking for Jo-Jo.

Bren had left for the muster camp soon after Neil's car drove away. Luci sat on the verandah reading glossy fashion magazines. She did not look up as Vienna headed down towards the garden, but Vienna had the distinct impression that Luci noticed every move she made.

Abby hadn't waited around to say goodbye to Neil and Myra. There were more quarrions at the waterhole, she said, and she wanted to sketch them before they flew away.

Terry worked in the sheds, re-doing the temporary repair on the Range Rover. Jo-Jo was nowhere in the garden.

Vienna kept walking. She couldn't settle. Neil's departure had meant the cutting of some kind of lifeline. She was truly on her own now. Never again would she knock on the Administrator's door at the nursing home and wait for the lift of Neil's handsome head with eagerness. It was all over. Whatever happened in her life now, Neil would have no part in it.

Restlessly, she wandered through the citrus trees and down to the home paddocks; and when Bren came out of the heat haze, riding the chestnut as he always did, she leaned her folded arms on the

slip-rails and watched him approach, with a weird
sense of not being in control of her own destiny.
She felt as though someone had written a script
and she was playing her part in it.

He pulled up, wheeling towards her, and as he
drew closer she saw that he looked as he always
did, confident and powerful and full of mockery.

He said, 'Waiting for me, Nursie?' and grinned
at her through the dust that streaked his face. He
swung himself down from the saddle, all the time
watching her, grey eyes intent. With a quick movement of one arm he indicated the gate, and she
opened it, being careful to close it behind her,
almost as if she were sleepwalking.

But as she walked closer to him she felt her
senses leap in response to his vitality. He made no
movement, only waited. A vibrance seemed to
spring to life between their two bodies, a height-
ened awareness that kept her moving closer to
him until she felt the heat from his body. His
eyes that she had thought so cool and distant
gleamed with a reckless promise of passion and
warmth. She was even conscious of the heartbeats
under the carelessly open shirt, as he waited for
her.

He breathed the strong deep breaths of a man
who has ridden hard and fast, and as she came
towards him, he held out both his arms wide for
her to walk into. Such arrogance! So very sure of
himself, he was. Crinkled eyes laughing down at
her, he waited. The sinews of the long, strong
throat showed taut as he threw back his head and
laughed at her, still holding out those waiting
arms.

Heaven knew what disaster might have followed,
what shameful capitulation might have swept her

away, if Abby had not chosen that moment to approach the paddocks.

She called, 'So there you are!' and her clear light voice jolted Vienna back to reality.

Vienna exclaimed, 'Abby!' and the man lowered his arms. He wasn't at all perturbed. If not today, his laughing face promised, there's always tomorrow . . .

'We have endless time,' he was saying. 'Endless time between us. There's no hurry.'

But it wasn't true. Nobody had endless time. Just because he moved in vast dimensions, surrounded by space that seemed to stretch for ever, in a land where history was measured from the beginnings of time, he didn't realise how short a time they had.

He shrugged and turned away to attend to his horse, and Vienna felt afraid because of his lack of urgency. If he felt like she did, surely he could not have set the moment aside so casually.

She walked back to the homestead with Abby, her emotions in turmoil. That had been a near escape. She had been so close—so very close—to surrender. Even now, the thought of those waiting arms made her body tingle, but she smothered the memory.

For what had he been proposing? A dalliance that might as well take place tomorrow as today? A passionate interlude that would have left her forever tender to the touch of love?

In a half-dream, Vienna moved through what remained of the afternoon.

Luci appeared in startling aquamarine for dinner, a long graceful gown that set her scintillating more brightly than ever. Vienna wore the cream skirt, the cream and gold patterned blouse, now

repaired painstakingly with needle and thread
borrowed from Dorothy Green.

She withdrew herself purposefully from them all,
sitting quietly and listening to Abby's chatter, letting their voices flow around her, answering in
monosyllables, politely, without involving herself.
She ought to have gone home with Neil instead of
staying here in this explosive situation that could
so easily turn out too much for her to handle.

After dinner, she left the clearing away for
Noreen and Jenny and walked in the garden, because that was what she needed tonight—the protective darkness around her like a security blanket,
the perfumed trees and creepers rustling, soothing
away dejection.

'I've been very stupid.' She almost spoke it
aloud. Because she *had* been stupid ... allowing a
painting to throw her off balance so that she
followed a dream into the outback wilderness and
got herself properly punished for her rashness.

'I can see you there,' Evelyn Harryn had insisted,
but Evelyn could have had no premonition of the
anguish it would bring her.

Vienna walked across the shadows of the travel-
lers palms to the bougainvillaea summerhouse.
Inside it, the folded chairs and recliners reproached
with their emptiness. Everything was unoccupied.
The sounds in the trees were only wind-rustling.
There were no night birds making mysterious hunt-
ing-calls, no small dartings of nocturnal animals.
Everything empty.

Until the faint crunch of feet on the gritty path,
the quick confident steps of the master of Glenister
Two, coming up behind her.

She twisted away, but he was too quick for her.
He slid an arm around her waist, pulling her back-

wards and close to him, holding her against his body.

'I always seem to be creeping up behind you. Had you noticed?'

'Yes.' Of course she'd noticed. What did he think she was made of—sand and stone?

She wanted to be face to face with him when she launched her question, so that he could not evade it; but he held her immobile, so she asked it of the empty summerhouse.

'Why do you bother?'

'If you mean why tonight, I'm here because I have something to ask you, something that happens to be very important to me.'

'So ask,' she said. But she wished he wouldn't stand so near. His arms held her like steel bands. Her body moved with his breathing.

He said, 'You took yourself away from me this afternoon, Sister Maddern. One minute you were standing there, with your eyes full of love, and your lips—your lips asking—— And I thought, yes, she wants me. Then you switched it all off. Like tonight. Why? For God's sake, what happened?' His hands moved to her shoulders, his fingers curling into soft flesh. He muttered huskily, 'I thought you might like to explain.'

Vienna's throat choked with pain. She touched dry lips with her tongue, and the words stumbled out reluctantly.

'I—I don't want—an affair with you.'

His arms tightened painfully.

'Who said anything about an affair?'

He let her turn then, pressing her against him so her head was pillowed on his chest. Her dark glossy hair brushed his jaw. He moved his face against its softness. But she pulled her head away from his seduction, her eyes large and brilliant.

'You mean, that's not what you have in mind? An affair?' Her voice was incredulous.

Again the flash of white smile in darkness, but he kept his large strong hands firmly around her.

'I'll tell you the truth, Nurse,' he admitted, with mock solemnity. 'I maybe did have that in mind at one time. In the beginning——' He was keeping it light, smiling down at her almost casually, but the arms around her were trembling. 'I thought you were living with that—that pretentious young pup. He led me to believe so. And I wanted to kill him even then, the first time I saw you, to take his neck in my hands and wring it. Then, when he grabbed at the opportunity to look at that land—at Red Vistas—I saw your face.' He bent his head and touched the dark wings of her hair with his cheek. 'I did—*then*, I admit it. I thought, Now—now while she's being disillusioned, while she's seeing him the way he really is—this could be my chance. I said to myself, You might take her now, if you're smart.'

He silenced her indignant protests with his lips, moving his head so that their lips brushed together softly, and Vienna felt herself capitulating, wanting him, needing to be swept away in the wave of feeling that had almost taken her away that afternoon.

Slowly he lifted his head. 'So I was cynical,' he said. 'So I'm sorry.' He trailed a fingertip lightly, feather-lightly, across her throat. 'And then,' he drew a deep relieving breath, 'then I realised, Miss Maddern, that you were a lot more innocent than I expected. That Mr Neil Rensome wasn't half as sure of you as he tried to make out. And I knew I wanted you for more than just a couple of months or a year. I want to grow old alongside you, to protect you, to share with you.'

His voice was deep and rich with feeling. Gently, he took her face in his hands and tilted it, so that he could study every feature, every curve and every hollow, and his lips made small swift contact with her forehead and eyelids, before they settled on her mouth, and he was stirring up waves of feeling again.

He had enough control for both of them. He held her carefully, head pillowed below his shoulder, and then he said, 'I want you in so many ways, my love. Not just in bed, though heaven knows I want that badly enough, but I have to know you'll be walking in the garden when I ride home, that I'll hear your voice and your footsteps in the homestead . . . Of course I want an affair with you,' he added. 'A permanent affair, one that will last the rest of our lives. A legal one. Could you see yourself, some day, being my wife? Loving me in all those ways?'

Vienna touched his face with her fingers, tracing the lines that told of strength and will and power, the sensuous mouth promising love and passion.

'All that and more,' she promised.

Bren said, 'You love me too? You feel the way I feel?' and there was wonder in his voice.

The scented garden rustled. The stars pulsed silver-bright.

His face softened as she lifted her arms and clasped them around his neck, so that his hairline made soft silk under her fingers. His eyes, that she had once thought cold, were bright with love.

'An affair!' he murmured, tracing the shape of her mouth with his finger. 'You must have known I wanted you for more than that.'

'How could I know?' she protested passionately.

'You never even said my name. You were so careful never to use it. Sister Maddern, you said. Miss Maddern. And that—that odious Nursie—— Never my one real name.'

Bren slid his fingers through her hair and turned the two dark wings into a soft cloud that fell around her shoulders. He loosened the buttons of the cream and gold blouse, and she felt the texture of his fingers as he caressed her shoulders free of straps.

'I was saving it,' he murmured, his voice as caressing as his fingertips.

'Saving it for what?'

'For this!'

As he bent his head she felt again the flutter of his breath against her cheek, then the swift cool contact of his lips against her ear.

'Vienna,' he murmured huskily; and the sound was music.